It isn't happy trails in South Lake Tahoe when newshound Elsie MacBean and her basset hound, Cruiser, stumble on the remains of Tallis Corporation CEO Chick Robson while hiking near Cave Rock.

Cave Rock, sacred ground to the Washoe Indians, is the proposed building site for fabulous new Cave Rock Resort and Casino, which promises to boost South Tahoe's sagging economy. Half-Washoe Beanie and the militant faction of the tribal council are forever at opposite ends of the totem pole on Native American issues in the Tahoe basin. When protests against Tallis turn murderous and Beanie's friend, Sheriff Skip Cassidy, asks her to help him solve the case, she's caught between a rock and a hard place. Evidence points to Tribal Elder Dan Silvernail, but Beanie and her slobbery sleuthhound dig up convincing clues to the contrary.

As the body count rises, a terrorized Tahoe community howls for the killer to be collared. It's up to Beanie and Cruiser to sniff out a deadly quarry before Tahoe goes to the dogs.

D0754076

M

HOWLING BLOODY MURDER

A Beanie and Cruiser Mystery

by

Sue Owens Wright

To the readers
of Woodland —
Thank you for inviting me.

Sue Owens Wright

Deadly Alibi Press Ltd.
PO Box 5947
Vancouver, WA 98661-5947

Disclaimer:
This book is a work of fiction. All characters and incidents mentioned herein are figments of the author's imagination. Any resem-
blance to actual events, locales or persons, living or dead, is en-
tirely coincidental.

For Tracy, Jean, Rhonda and everyone who encouraged and supported me along the way. "If your heart is in your dream, no request is too extreme."

Chapter One

A phone call from my daughter, Wenona, seemed to herald the reign of terror in our peaceful alpine valley of Lake Tahoe. South Shore buzzed about the controversy surrounding the death of a climber who fell from Cave Rock. The fatality was deemed accidental, but the condition of the rock climber's body suggested there might have been more to it than originally thought. Everyone knew the Washoe Tribe decried the fact that their sacred places were being defiled, but no one was pointing any fingers. Not yet.

The week before Thanksgiving, I was doing a routine flea check on my basset hound, Cruiser, when the phone's shrill ring startled me.

"Hi, Mom! It's me." Nona's voice always sounds like wind chimes.

"Nona. What's it been, two years since I last heard from you?"

"Aw, come on, Mom. It's only been a couple of weeks."

"What's keeping you so busy these days?" I parted Cruiser's fur inch by hairy inch, hot on the trail of a particularly elusive flea.

"I landed another modeling assignment."

"Not bathing suits again?"

"Lingerie, actually."

"Underwear?" I accidentally yanked a clump of red fur along with the flea that prepared to feast on Cruiser's backside. He yelped, which was how I felt when Nona said, 'lingerie.'

"No, Mom, not underwear. Lingerie."

"Same thing, isn't it?"

"Not exactly."

"Really, Nona. What would Pop have said?"

Nona's tone softened at the mention of her father. "I hope he'd say he's proud of me." I echoed the heavy sigh at the other end of the line. "Relax, Mom. It's for Victoria's Secret, not Hustler. Besides, I'm getting paid very well."

I worried that those photos might not be the only things being overexposed.

"Are you saving some of that money to come and see me and Cruiser during the holidays?" Cruiser's long ears perked up—no small feat for a basset—at the mention of his name, although I think he must have sensed the anticipation in my voice.

"How do you do it, Mom? Dad always said you were psychic. I think he was right."

"You mean you are coming?"

"Yes."

To heck with fleas, Nona was coming to visit! Cruiser sighed with relief when I lost interest in the search.

"That's great, honey. When?"

"I should be up on Tuesday."

"You'll be staying for Thanksgiving?" I held my breath. Nona's modeling career kept her so busy, we rarely had any quality time together.

"I have some time off after this job is finished. I'll stay longer, if that's all right with you."

I squealed with delight and hugged Cruiser. "Of course, it's all right with me."

"Um, there's just one thing..."

"What?"

"Can I bring my new boyfriend over for Thanksgiving dinner?"

Oh, no. Not another one, I thought. I loosened my grip on Cruiser's neck when he started to gag. "Who is it this time?"

"His name is Medwyn. Medwyn Abercarn."

For a moment, I couldn't make my tongue work. "You're joking. Right?"

"No, Mom."

"Medwyn Aber...Abraca...I can't even say it!"

"A-ber-carn. It's a Celtic name."

Great! Now Nona's dating Druids. I tried to picture my mystery guest. Halloween might have been a better time to meet Nona's boyfriend.

"Mom? You still there?"

"Yes."

"So, you don't mind if Medwyn comes to dinner?"

"Oh, well," I sighed. "I suppose not."

"Thanks, Mom. You're an angel."

"I'll tell a couple of Grandpop's stories, then we'll see if he passes the test."

"No, not that! I'll never see Meddy again!"

"Oh, all right. Don't get your lingerie in a bunch. What time will you be here?"

"I should make it by six, traffic permitting. I'll pick Medwyn up, and we'll be over later."

"He lives here in Tahoe?"

"Yes. We met at the Alpen Sierra coffee shop last time I visited. We're having dinner at the Fresh Ketch. I thought maybe we could stop by afterwards for coffee, so you two can get acquainted."

"Whatever." Sheesh! It seems like I see the glamour queen less and less these days. You'd think I could have her to myself for at least an hour.

"Well, gotta go. See you Tuesday. I'll phone you from the car if I'm running late."

"You have a cellular phone?"

"Uh, huh. Doesn't everyone?"

"No, not quite everyone." I'm one of the few people left who still steers her car with two hands. "I'll see you then, dear. Drive carefully, and don't forget to bring your skis. We can do some cross-country while you're here."

"You're on, Mom. 'Bye."

"Love you, Nonie."

"Me, too."

When I hung up the phone, I wished Nona were already here. I love the solace of the forest, but this cabin gets too quiet at times, even for me. I needed to talk to someone without four paws and floppy ears.

I could hardly wait for Nona's arrival. Odd boyfriends notwithstanding, I knew we'd have a wonderful time together, as always. Although we disagree from time to time, deep down Nona and I have always been soul mates.

But Nona wouldn't be caught dead wearing my Sherlock Holmes deerstalker. You know, the kind with funny earflaps that make you look like a cartoon hound dog. Only mine is a pinkish plaid. The MacBean tartan hat belonged to my husband, Tom. I wear it now that he's gone. Admittedly, it's strange attire for a woman who's half Washoe Indian. I'm also of English ancestry, which probably explains my penchant for deerstalkers and Doyle's master sleuth. If Sherlock had known Cruiser, he would have given Watson his walking papers. He's been my closest companion since Tom died battling a forest fire on Kingsbury Grade. I would never have made it through last winter if it weren't for Cruiser. That was when Cruiser and I had our adventure of a lifetime, and I'm not talking dog years.

By the way, I'm Elsinore MacBean. That's Elsie for short, but my friends call me Beanie, partly for the hat but also because of my industrial-strength vegetarian chili, guaranteed to send you sprinting for the nearest water fountain. I'm a storyteller, like my Washoe grandfather, and an amateur sleuth of sorts.

I once planned a career in law enforcement and studied criminology in college two years before landing a summer reporter's job with the San Francisco Chronicle. That sparked my love for writing and life in publishing's fast lane doing power lunches. But I was much younger then. These days, I settle for freelancing and a bowl of killer chili.

When I'm not getting myself entangled in Washoe tribal politics or stringing articles for the Tahoe Times or Fur and Feather Quarterly, I occasionally assist my good friend, Deputy Sheriff Skipper Cassidy, on unusual cases in South Lake Tahoe. My experiences with Skip have provided me with enough fodder for a great mystery novel, when I get around to writing it.

Christmas was still over a month away, but with Thanksgiving so close at hand, I considered it officially the holiday season and time to decorate the house from foundation to chimney pot. By the time my daughter arrived with Medwyn Whoozits, this place would look like a Thomas Kincade painting. Even Cruiser could get into the act. I still had those silly antlers he wore when I had his photo taken with Santa Paws one year at the local pet shop, The Haute Hydrant.

I found all but one box of Christmas decorations in my attic. I must have loaned it to Nona the year she wanted to deck the tiny halls of her first apartment. I pulled out the matted ball of twinkle lights I had tossed in the box last year after I pulled them off the pine tree beside the driveway. I could see this might take awhile, so I clicked the television on, made a nice cup of cocoa and sat down on the couch to undertake Tom's traditional holiday task I'd inherited. I unraveled the lights one by one, cursing under my breath.

"We join Anchor Heather Halloran live at Cave Rock, the site of a rock climber's recent death, where a demonstration is in progress," said the news commentator. "Heather?"

"Thank you, Randy. I'm here at Cave Rock, a sacred spot to the Washoe Indians, where a group of tribal members, led by Sonseah Little Feather and Dan Silvernail, are gathered to protest the recent ground breaking for Cave Rock Casino and Resort being built by Tallis Corporation," Heather said. "The new recreational playground is being designed to incorporate the massive rock into a year-round, indoor/outdoor rock-climbers' facility."

I had to admit that in spite of the fact Sonseah is my age, she looked great, and TV always adds 10 pounds. She wore native dress to the protest, for effect. Never mind the fact that she drives a late model bimer and shops at upscale Tahoe boutiques, thanks to Indian gaming profits, which added fresh fuel to the bonfire that still smolders between Indians and Whites.

Dan Silvernail flanked Sonseah, wearing his long hair tied back under his trademark black Stetson. A quill from the endangered bald eagle decorated its brim. Both Dan and Sonseah are revered tribal elders. I am also concerned about anything that affects our people and was no greater fan of Tallis than they, but we have slightly different views on Native American affairs in the Tahoe Basin. We're forever finding ourselves on opposing ends of the totem pole.

"We will fight to keep the rock climbers and Tallis Corporation from further desecrating Cave Rock, our spiritual stronghold," Sonseah said to the reporter. "As long as they continue to defile it and mock us with names such as "Psycho Monkey," which they give the routes used to climb the rock, we will stand as a nation to save our civilization, as we should have 100 years ago when we were driven away from our land by the white man."

"Sonseah's on her soapbox again, Cruiser," I mumbled while untangling twinkle lights, most of which wouldn't twinkle.

Cruiser ambled up and sniffed the open box of decorations. Discovering no biscuits inside, he curled up beside the fire on his favorite pillow, the one generously coated with dog hair.

"Looks like Tallis CEO Richard Brennan is also here. Let's see if we can't get a word with him," Heather said, sidling up to the CEO who looked like he'd just stepped off the cover of Gentlemen's Quarterly. "Mr. Brennan, excuse me. Would you care to comment on Ms. Little Feather's statement?"

Brennan stepped to the mike. "Cave Rock Resort is going to boost the sagging economy in Tahoe like you've never seen. Rock-climbing is becoming a very popular sport. The draw to this spectacular new attraction and casino will be phenomenal, bringing more tourists to the area. That's good news for everyone, including the Indians. As far as we're concerned, it's full steam ahead on this newest Tallis project."

"How will your new casino help the Washoe, unless we're running it?" Dan Silvernail retorted off-camera.

"Does that mean construction will continue through the winter?" continued Heather.

"Yes, as weather permits, of course. With the drought conditions, we shouldn't encounter many delays. We've already had far too many delays on this project as it is." Brennan shot a defiant look at Sonseah and Dan. "We intend to have Cave Rock Resort up and running by summer."

"Save Cave Rock! Save Cave Rock!" The protesters began chanting, drowning out Heather's interview.

"Well, uh, thank you, Mr. Brennan, for your time," Heather shouted over the din. "Back to you, Randy!"

"Thank you, Heather. And now, on to the weather..."

Randy laughed at his newsy pun.

I soon found my mind wandering back to the task at hand. I thought of many things while sorting decorations. My thoughts turned to Tom as I unwrapped the first ornament we had ever purchased together, a silver heart engraved "Christmas 1971," the year we were married. Here I was, facing another holiday without him.

The year following his death was the hardest I'd ever had to bear. Loneliness took on a new meaning. I blamed myself for his death because I had wanted this peeled cedar cabin with knotty pine walls nestled in Tahoe National Forest. It was my dream, not Tom's, that brought us here.

As I admired the Baby's First Christmas ornament my parents gave us after Nona's birth, I heard the mournful wail rising from somewhere in the forest. The unearthly ululation made the hairs on my neck spike. Cruiser heard it too, for he woke suddenly from his comfortable slumber, sat upright on his haunches, and bayed in answer to the feral lament.

Chapter Two

Early the morning after Nona's call, I awoke with a start for the second time in a week, my heart hammering. The lamp shade beside my bed was jiggling. Could it be another Markleeville earthquake? Probably Tallis doing more blasting at Cave Rock.

Then I felt the crushing weight on my chest. I knew I wasn't having a heart attack when a wet tongue lapped my cheek. An alarm clock is unnecessary when an 80-pound hound sleeps at the foot of the bed. I usually get a six o'clock wake-up call, or earlier if I forget to let him out at bedtime. This time the tremors woke us both.

"Cruiser, what's the matter, fella? You all shook up, too?" I stroked his soft fur and felt my pulse rate drop.

After an appreciative lick on my chin, Cruiser jumped down from the bed and headed for the front door. When I opened the door, I glanced around just to be sure everything looked normal before I gave Cruiser the "potty time" command. I don't scare easily, but to tell you the truth, I was spooked by the sound I had heard the night before, and I worried that Cruiser might wander off and get into trouble, as scent hounds are inclined to do.

Coyotes are among the creatures that inhabit the woods. They sing me to sleep many nights as I lie awake in bed brainstorming my articles and the mystery novel I'll write some day. Although a lone coyote would probably shy away from Cruiser, a pack might be bold enough to attack. Small game is scarce during frigid winter months. A neighbor lost her poodle that way. Left chained on her porch, the poor thing ended up as a canine canapé. But it wasn't a coyote I'd heard, and it wasn't a cougar. It wasn't a sound I'd ever heard, and that's what worried me. Apparently, it worried

Cruiser, too, because when I gave the potty command, he refused to go outside.

"It's all right, boy. We'll try again later."

Cruiser followed close at my heels as I stepped into the bathroom to rinse the sleep from my eyes. I plugged the drain and twisted the faucet. While the basin filled, I soaked a washcloth with warm water and worked up a soapy lather. After a good scrubbing and rinsing, I patted my face dry with a towel. The plump, perimenopausal woman in the mirror stared back at me with the cinnamon-colored eyes of my mother, framed in dark circles from a restless night's sleep. Where was the girl I used to be? My double chin reminded me of Cruiser's dewlaps.

"Looks like we could both use a facelift, huh, boy?"

Cruiser shook his pendulous flews, flipping saliva on the shower curtain. I chuckled as I remembered how much that once had annoyed Tom.

Tom was never much of a dog person. He grew up in his widowed mother's Tiburon houseful of finicky felines. But it wasn't long after Tom found Cruiser abandoned on the roadside by uncaring tourists that the two of them bonded. Cruiser's nap in Tom's lap that first evening was the coup de grâce. Tom stroked the stray dog's head, unaware his clean slacks were being soaked with drool from Cruiser's chin—a sort of basset baptism. After that, Cruiser was ours for keeps.

During the following months, ex-cat fancier Tom MacBean learned to tolerate the muddy paw prints and slobber stains. Not long before Tom died, he built a sun deck, something appreciated on chilly Tahoe mornings, especially by a certain sun-loving basset who loves to turn his downside up to the tongue-lolling warmth. Tom claimed he built the deck for my sunbathing, but we both knew who he really built it for.

I raked a comb through my hair, tracing a crooked part down the center of my scalp. Plaiting a long braid at each ear, I tossed them over my shoulders like lassos.

"So you're not as young as you used to be," I consoled myself. Even though the sand in the hourglass had shifted a bit (Scotsman Tom called my ample figure "bonnie"), and silver threads streaked my sable hair, I was still attractive to the opposite sex. I could turn a head or two if I had a mind to, even if I was entering "The Pause."

"Age is just mind over matter; if you don't mind, it doesn't matter. Right, Cruiser? Cruiser?" I heard a familiar scratching at the door. I yanked on my Sunday morning leisure suit, which consists of torn Levi's and a faded "I Love Tahoe" sweatshirt. I let Cruiser out to water his favorite pine tree. This time he shot straight out the door. I brewed French Roast coffee and boiled some oatmeal for breakfast. By the time the oatmeal was ready, I heard Cruiser scratching at the door to be let in.

"Well, that didn't take long, did it? What's the matter, boy? Get cold paws?" When I opened the door, Cruiser dropped a souvenir of his outing at my feet, then made a beeline for his food dish. His eyes were two question marks when he found it empty. He let out a baritone bark.

"All right. Keep your hair suit on, will ya?" I reached down to retrieve the strange object at my feet. "Aaagh!" Cruiser looked insulted when I screeched and dropped his trophy. It hit the floor with a thud. "What the heck is this, a rat?" Then I realized it wasn't a rat, but the hind leg of a jackrabbit. Torn, bloodied ligaments hung from the severed appendage like spaghetti in marinara sauce.

"Looks like Thumper had a really bad day in the forest." I tossed Cruiser's grisly keepsake in the garbage can outside the back door. "Thanks, Cruiser. Next time you find something disgusting, please leave it where you found it." I knew I'd better keep a closer eye on Cruiser with predators close by. They might prefer a basset to Bugs Bunny.

I dumped a moderate helping of expensive diet dog food into Cruiser's dish from the 40-pound bag I'd bought from the vet the day before. Doc Heaton wasn't pleased with Cruiser's weigh-in. If only there were a Jenny Craig for dogs.

Cruiser sniffed at his dish before sampling the diet kibble. He gummed the food once or twice before depositing it in a slobbery wad on the floor.

"Come on, boy," I said, getting down on all fours beside the dish labeled Top Dog. "Lookie here! Mmmm. Yummy, wummy for Cruiser's tummy." He looked at me as though I'd sprouted green dog biscuits from my ears.

"Cruiser, you eat this right now!" I grumbled, pointing at his bowl. He grumbled right back as he waddled off and flopped down on the opposite side of the kitchen, huffing his displeasure and giving me *the look*.

"All right, then. Have it your way. Maybe this will taste better to you tonight. And no dog treats for you today, young man," I decreed and removed his dish. It was hard to be firm with him, but I had to for his own good. I would take him for a long walk later, but first I had some errands to run.

I needed to pick up tickets for the Firemen's Association Ball & Fund-raiser. I asked Skip if he would accompany me to the ball, since Cruiser wouldn't do as my escort. I knew Skip wouldn't refuse. He was Tom's best friend, and Skip and I have become close friends since Tom died.

I don't go out on dates much. It's not for lack of invitations. I guess I'm just not ready to get seriously involved with anyone yet. Escorted or not, I always attend the Firemen's Ball, as I did every year with Tom. In more than one way he was a rare man, one who loved to dance. We even took lessons together at Arthur Murray.

On our first date, Tom took me to the Tartan Ball in San Francisco, back in the swinging sixties. My best friend, Molly, had arranged a blind date, and I was a nervous wreck. When Tom showed up at the door wearing a kilt and a badger sporran, I vowed to get even with her. She was always setting me up with dates, most of them ending in disaster. That first date with Tom was no exception, but not because of the plaid skirt or the dead badger (I was the one out of place at the ball with my Dayglo miniskirt and white vinyl go-go boots). As I recall, it had something to do with haggis and hurling.

Of course, my views on eating meat are not shared by my roomie. I'm sure a nice hunk of haggis would have been right up a certain picky basset's alley. I gulped down the last of my coffee, made myself presentable, and grabbed Cruiser's leash from the hall tree.

"Come on, Cruiser. Let's go for a ride," I said, jangling the tags on his collar like sleigh bells. The only thing besides food that will lure Cruiser from his hairy pillow is a ride in the car, which is why we named him Cruiser. Hanging his head out the window, he catches all the interesting smells. Everyone recognizes my car. It's the one with long ears flapping in the breeze.

I hefted Cruiser into his copilot's seat, and we were off. I steered the Jeep onto Pioneer Trail and headed for Elks Club Drive. I stopped by to see Jim Meecham at Lake Tahoe Wildlife Rescue where I dropped off an article for their next newsletter issue of Fur and Feather Quarterly. I'd spent the last two weeks researching a story on illegal dog fighting. Rumors were flying that a ring was operating in South Tahoe, but neither I nor the local Humane Society had yet managed to find out where.

"Hey, there, Beanie. What's cookin'?" Jim said, looking up momentarily from some paperwork when he saw me come in.

"Not much."

"Not even that famous spicy chili of yours?"

"No one's eyes are watering at the moment. What's new with you, Jim?"

"Had another casualty last night," he said, his expression grim.

"What was it this time?" An animal in distress is always bad news.

"A fawn—hit by a car."

"Poor thing."

"We didn't find the doe. She's probably dead."

"The fawn survive?"

"We got to the little fella just in time, but he'll be a long time mending."

"Anything I can do to help?"

"Thanks, but Connie and I can handle this one."

Jim and I had been friends since I appeared at his door one morning with an injured ground squirrel, another victim of a car. Jim and his wife, Connie, nursed it back to health. They even invited me along for its release into the wild, far away from busy streets.

Jim pushed his papers aside. "Now, what can I do for you, Beanie?"

I handed him the article I'd written.

Jim smiled. "Great, thanks!"

"Any idea what you want to cover in the next issue?"

"Sure do. We've been finding a lot of dead game in the area lately."

"Poachers, you think?"

"Could be. We're not sure. If it is, they aren't using guns. Too messy for that."

I gulped, recalling Cruiser's sickening trophy.

"Cruiser found what was left of some poor rabbit this morning."

"Another one? Could be some kind of weird sacrificial cult. It will be cats and dogs next, like in Sacramento."

"It's probably just a pack of coyotes, don't you think? Tourists won't stop feeding them, so they're moving in closer to civilization. They carried off a few cats and a small dog last summer in my neighborhood."

"Possibly, but we need to alert pet owners about the problem, just in case."

"I'll get on it right away."

"Thanks, Beanie."

Had poachers killed the rabbit near my cabin? A Satanic cult? Or something else? As I drove away, Jim's words sounded a tiny alarm in my head, but apparently I had gone tone deaf. I suppose I just had too much on my mind with Nona visiting. I'd have to stock the larder before she and her boyfriend arrived for Thanksgiving. The cupboard can get pretty bare when you're cooking for one. But I never run out of chocolate chip cookies...or dog biscuits. Cruiser would be the first one to let Mother Hubbard know about that.

When I reached the "Y" at the junction of Highway 50 and 89, I stopped first at the Sierra Bookshop to pick up the new volume of Writer's Market, then popped into Raley's to buy some groceries and a bag of chocolate chip cookies, carefully placing them out of Cruiser's reach. I diverted his attention with a new rawhide chewy, which he went right to work on.

As I drove up Al Tahoe Boulevard, the majestic Sierras were a picture postcard view. Snow caps from the first dusting of snow shimmered in the morning sun. The sky was brilliant sapphire, the color of my Tom's eyes. Swollen, gray clouds brushing the peaks signaled a storm approached, the first of the season. Hooray! Nona and I would have snow for skiing.

    Turning onto Pioneer Trail, I spotted Skip's patrol car speeding in the opposite direction. I waved, but he apparently didn't see me. As we passed each other, his car's warning lights began flashing, the siren shrieking. He was hot on the trail of something, and I had a fleeting urge to join the chase. What I didn't know then was that all too soon Cruiser and I would find ourselves on a trail headed for trouble.

Chapter Three

"Just one more stop, Cruiser, then home," I assured my restless passenger as I pulled into the driveway of the fire station. When I hopped out of the car and headed for the office, I saw freshly washed in the garage the red fire engine Tom rode in to his last forest fire. Her grill glistened like tinsel in the morning sun. She looked so festive, I nearly managed to blot out the sad memories of Tom's tragic death.

I jumped when I heard someone holler, "Hi, Beanie!" I hadn't noticed Fire Chief Bob Baker crouched at the rear of the fire truck busily polishing the chrome bumper. He stood up and wiped his hands with a rag.

"Oh! Hi ya, Bob." I quickly brushed away my tears before he could see I'd been crying.

"Where's that bruiser, Cruiser?"

"He's waiting in the car."

"You didn't bring him in to say hi to Uncle Bob?"

"Next time. I just dropped by to pick up the tickets for the Firemen's Ball. You got a couple for me lying around here somewhere?"

"You betcha! Come right this way." I followed Bob to his office. He lifted a metal tackle box from a desk drawer, and plunked it down.

"Did you say two?"

"Yes."

"Who's the lucky fella?" Bob's friendly brown eyes met mine for a moment. They looked almost as baleful as Cruiser's when I answered.

"Skip Cassidy."

Bob quickly averted his gaze and opened the box, which smelled faintly of fish bait.

"Oh. Hopalong, eh?"

Skip, a first-class lawman, earned the unfortunate nickname of Hopalong Cassidy when he accidentally shot himself in the foot at rookie target practice and had managed to hop all the way to the infirmary.

"Do I taste some sour grapes here, Bob?"

"Nah. Only, how about giving me dibs on a date sometime?"

"But I thought you and Rita were still a hot item?"

"Not anymore. We broke up a couple of months ago. She's dating the sheriff now."

"Mike Stoddard?"

"Yep."

"Last night my daughter told me she broke up with her old boyfriend, too. It must be catching."

"Wenona's a very attractive young lady. I suppose she has to fight the guys off with a stick."

"In San Francisco? Are you kidding? Anyway, if that's the case, how did she end up with some dweeb named Medwyn Abercarn?"

"Medwyn who?"

"That's what I said."

"Is she coming up for Thanksgiving?"

"Yes. And guess who she's bringing along?"

"Medwyn?"

"Uh, huh."

"Well, here's your chance to check him out. You never know. He might be a weirdo or something."

"She's brought home plenty of weirdoes before. The last guy she dated wore a ring in his nose and a few other places I'd rather not mention."

I made a joke of it, like I do about most things, but the truth was Nona's life choices lately had me genuinely concerned for her welfare.

Bob guffawed. "Say, maybe you should buy two extra tickets, just in case they want to join you."

"Hey, you're right. The dance is next Saturday. They'll still be here." *That way I can keep an eye on them.* "Okay, make it four tickets. How much do I owe you?"

"That'll be a hundred even."

"A hundred dollars! Have the tickets gone up that much since last year?"

"'Fraid so. But remember, it's for sweet charity."

"I know. Tom and I always supported The Firemen's Association. I don't plan to stop now." I counted out five twenties. Suddenly concerned about Cruiser, I turned toward the door. "Well, gotta run. I have an 80-pound charity out in the car who probably has a full tank."

"Wait, Beanie! Your tickets."

"Oh, yeah. Almost forgot."

"Have a nice Thanksgiving."

"Thanks, Bob. You, too."

Well, where the heck have you been for so long? Cruiser seemed to demand, then ignored me, like he always has when left behind. Once he snubbed me for a whole week after Tom and I returned from our two-week vacation abroad one summer. Not Tom; just me, as though it were all my idea to leave him in a kennel. Never mind that it was a virtual hound dog Hilton. Since then, I hire a house sitter whenever I travel, a lovely little Scottish lady who coincidentally goes by the name, Scotty. Anytime I'm called away on a writing assignment, she stays with Cruiser. They get along famously, and she spoils him worse than I do, which is probably why he doesn't pay much attention to me when I return.

The moment I pulled into my driveway and opened the passenger door, Cruiser leaped out. Ever seen a basset hound leap, or an elephant fly? He waddled up to his favorite watering post, the old sugar pine, and did a three-legged ballet. Cruiser's never been the hydrant type. He never does anything in a small way. I've seen him nearly do a back flip trying to mark the 30-foot pine tree in my front yard. He wants his rivals to know he's still top dog around here, like the food dish says. As high as I've seen him piddle up that tree, the other dogs probably think I have a pet giraffe. I've considered cutting notches in the bark to see if any of the other dogs can break his record. A kind of Doggy Olympics, if you will.

Having completed his mission impossible, Cruiser followed me into the house, no doubt hoping for a mid-morning snack. Instead, he was in for some serious exercise—doctor's orders. I stashed the groceries and snatched his leash from the hall tree. "Come on, Cruiser. Walkies, boy!"

I had said the magic word. I snapped the leash to

his collar, and we headed up the meandering trail into the woods. My mother and I often hiked that trail in the months before she died.

The wind whisking through the quaking aspens, their leaves softly clattering like a ceremonial rattle, is Momma's gentle voice. I feel her fingers brush through my hair and her soft caress upon my upturned face. Her presence is everywhere around me, speaking through the benevolent spirits of the woods.

A great tree, probably one of the few that survived the logging frenzy of the 1800s, stands in the clearing at the crest of the mountain. I call it the hugging tree. When I wrap my arms around this tree, I draw energy from its life force, and I feel at peace.

On this particular day, I stood in the clearing with Cruiser. I was hugging my tree, Cruiser hugging his. We were as content as human and canine can possibly be. In fact, I didn't even notice Cruiser doing his famous disappearing act. He followed his nose first from one cluster of manzanita, then to the next. Minutes later I heard a sound, but it wasn't what I'd heard the night before. This sound was familiar. It was Cruiser! What had that dog gotten into now?

I ran in the direction of the commotion. Had coyotes attacked him? Was he caught in a poacher's trap? Horrible images flashed through my head as I zigzagged between manzanita bushes stabbing at my legs. None of the dreadful thoughts I imagined could ever have matched what I found when I came upon Cruiser, howling like a banshee.

Chapter Four

Tuesday morning at Debbie's Diner I sat in my favorite corner booth reading the Tahoe Times. My eyes locked on the headline grabber, **"LOCAL DEVELOPER FOUND DEAD ON RIM TRAIL."** I read on. "Tallis Executive, Robert 'Chick' Robson's mutilated remains were discovered yesterday near Cave Rock on a popular hiking trail by a local woman and her dog. The murder is currently under investigation. Anyone having any information pertaining to this crime should call 555-TAHO."

"Here's your veggie omelet, no onions," said petite, busty waitress, Rita Ramirez. "More coffee?"

"Uh, no. Not right now, thanks." I wondered why she didn't move on to the next booth. I noticed her scanning the headlines.

"Did you write that?"

"Nope." I scooped up a generous helping of omelet with my fork and aimed it for my mouth, hoping she would take the hint and move along. She didn't.

"Isn't it awful about that guy the police found?" Rita said, snapping her gum and blowing a wayward strand of Lucille Ball crimson hair from her eyes. "They say he was quite a mess. Found pieces of him everywhere."

I felt my stomach lurch at the memory of what Cruiser and I found. Suddenly, I wondered why I'd ordered an omelet. I set down my fork and shot cinnamon daggers at her.

"Oops. Sorry." When Rita giggled in that annoying nasal way of hers, I knew she wasn't one bit sorry.

"Oh, Miss," called an elderly gent from a booth across the aisle. "More coffee, please."

"Coming right up," Rita said, hurrying off to the

waitress's station for the coffee pot.

Good riddance. I could resume reading my paper in peace. I pushed the plate away and sipped my coffee as I continued scanning the feature article. I turned to page A-8 to see a photo of Cruiser and me at the crime scene. "Jeez, I gotta go on a diet," I muttered. I waved to Rita to heat up my coffee. She didn't see me, or pretended not to, so I kept on reading. "Investigators found a shoe in the bushes near the body. Police have not yet determined if it belonged to the victim."

A thumbnail photo of Skip at the bottom of the page accompanied a pull-quote that read, "One officer at the crime scene commented, "Looks like Freddy Kruger Does Tahoe." Yep. That could come from none other than Mr. Skip "Hopalong" Cassidy. Maybe that's why we get along so well, because his warped sense of humor is so much like mine. For Skip, black humor serves as a release valve on sometimes difficult investigations, none of them more so than this one would turn out to be.

I couldn't help laughing. "Hah. Good one, Skip. Your boss will just love it."

"Well, you're dead wrong, Beanie," spoke a familiar voice.

I looked up into a pair of impish blue eyes belonging to none other than Deputy Skipper Cassidy. Stalks of straw blonde hair poked out from under his cap. That, his slender build and sunny smile made him resemble the scarecrow in "The Wizard of Oz." He often fools people with his Barney Fife manner, but Skip is a darned good cop, even if he had trouble convincing his nemesis, Sheriff Mike Stoddard. Of course, no one, including his boss, seemed to realize how much determination it must have taken for an injured and bleeding man to hop one-footed for half a mile. No one except me, apparently.

"Hi, Skip. Take a load off your loafers."

"Thanks. Don't mind if I do." Doffing his cap, Skip scooted into the seat opposite me. "I see your news hound made the papers."

"Yeah, there'll be no living with him now."

"Whadya mean *now*?" Skip laughed, until he glimpsed a photo of his boss on the back page.

"Stoddard wasn't too keen on the Freddy joke, eh?"

"You guessed right. When will I ever learn to button my lip?"

"He just doesn't appreciate your sense of humor."

"Maybe I should have saved it for later over a beer with the guys."

"I could have used one, too, after Cruiser sniffing out Robson yesterday on our walk. I nearly tossed my chocolate chip cookies."

"It was bad, all right. Here a Chick, there a Chick, everywhere a Chick, Chick."

"Any leads?"

"Not yet." Skip scratched his chin, like he always does when puzzled.

"The guy looked like he'd been through a Cuisinart." I shuddered as I thought again of the grisly sight of the victim's torn throat and torso, the look of terror frozen in his contorted features.

"Think it could have been some kind of animal?"

"Could be, I guess."

"A cougar, maybe?" Skip waved for the waitress.

"Maybe, unless..."

"What?"

"Freddy Kruger *is* doing Tahoe."

"In your nightmares, Beanie."

"Coffee, Deputy?" Rita broke in, making limpid goo-goo eyes at Skip, like she did with every man from Truckee to Twin Bridges.

He nodded and smiled the way men usually do with top-heavy, flirtatious waitresses. "Sure, Rita."

Rita leaned way over to pour the coffee. Skip's eyes popped.

"I'll have some more, too," I said.

Rita snapped her gum and poured my coffee, leaving brown dribble marks on my newspaper. "Oops, sorry."

"See anything you like, Skip?" I teased as Rita sashayed over to the old gent gumming his oatmeal in the booth across the aisle. I thought he might have a stroke when Rita leaned over to warm up his coffee cup. She warmed up more than his coffee. I could see steam forming on his trifocals from where I sat.

"Nah, she's not my type," he said, trying hard not to stare after he'd been caught in the act.
"Could've fooled me."

"I prefer older women." Skip winked at me.

"Gee, thanks a heap, Pal," I muttered. "Is there a plastic surgeon in the house?"

"Did you pick up the dance tickets yet?" He changed the subject, realizing his remark had cut a little deeper than he intended.

"Sure did. Four of them."

"Four? Who are the other two for?"

"My daughter and some guy she met."

"Oh, I didn't know we needed chaperones, Beanie."

"Don't be silly. I just thought that since Nona will be here for Thanksgiving, she might like to take her date out for a big night under the bright lights."

"This is Tahoe, not Vegas."

"Who could tell, with Rita dangling her tassels all over the place."

"Aw, you know Rita. She flirts with all the men like that. I'm nothing special."

"Well, you are to me."

Skip grinned like a frog that just swallowed the biggest bug in the pond.

"I don't let just anyone escort me to the Firemen's Ball, you know."

His eyes suddenly misted, "I know." He had grieved nearly as long as I over Tom's death. They were best friends for as long as we had lived in Tahoe, often golfing or fishing together on Skip's outboard, the Trout Scout.

"Hey, Fred. Where's that order of trout for Deputy Cassidy?" Rita squawked at the large, sweaty chef in the kitchen.

"Keep your blouse on, Rita. I think I see a school of them swimming by just about...NOW!" He flopped the butter-fried fish on a platter and scooted it across the counter.

When Rita set the trout before Skip, I crinkled my nose.

"What, no 'Moons over My Hammy,' Skip?"

"Wrong restaurant, Beanie."

"You're as bad as Tom with his kippered herring at

breakfast. I think this is my cue to leave." I gulped down the last of my coffee.

"Still not a fish fan, eh?"

"No, but how about joining me for a dish of my killer veggie chili tonight? I'll cook up a special batch just for you."

"Sounds mighty good. You'll put lots of onions in it for me?"

"Sure. A truckload, if you want."

"You're on. What time?"

"Let's make it seven o'clock, okay? I need to walk Cruiser first. He'll be glad to see you. He misses having another guy around the house."

"Yeah, sure. Seven's fine." A worried expression crossed Skip's face.

"What's wrong?" I asked.

"I'll tell you tonight when I see you."

The tone in his voice was uncharacteristically subdued, and I instinctively knew Skip was in trouble. I didn't know then just how much.

Chapter Five

When I got home, it was nearly lunchtime. I offered Cruiser some diet kibble, but he still pouted over the change in his menu. He sniffed at the kibble, then shoveled most of it out of the bowl and onto the floor, searching for tastier morsels before tailing me to the kitchen counter. I rustled up some lunch for myself from some leftover egg salad. As I arranged two slices of nine-grain bread on the cutting board, I became conscious of two eyes intently watching me. I dolloped on the mixture, and pressed the slices together. When I sat down at the kitchen table, Cruiser waddled over and plopped his sloppy jowls on my right knee, eyeing up my sandwich for the kill.

"No, boy. You're on a diet, remember?"

He didn't budge.

"Down, Cruiser. This is *my* sandwich."

I tried to ignore him, but it was no use. I was beginning to crack. He knew it. I knew it. It was just a matter of time...

"Oh, all right then. I'll get you a biscuit." I pushed his wet muzzle aside, wrung out my soggy pant leg and went to the pantry, otherwise known as Cruiser's yum-yum nook. Unlike Mother Hubbard's poor dog, this dog has a stash replenished weekly with every kind of bowser delight known to Dogdom. What would I do with all his doggie yum-yum's now that he was on a diet? I felt guilty giving him one against Doc's orders, but I'm putty in his paws.

I opened a box of dog biscuits. "Here you go, boy." He snapped up the treat like a crocodile in a sushi bar. In less than a nanosecond, all that remained of the biscuit were microscopic crumbs scattered on the floor. Cruiser's keen nose led him to each morsel, which he quickly vacuumed up. Why hadn't I named him Hoover?

I used the diversion to gobble up the last of my sandwich. I had just taken the last mouthful when the phone rang. Never fails! I forced down the final bite with a quick gulp of tea and dashed for the phone, hoping like crazy it wasn't Nona calling to say she couldn't make it for Thanksgiving after all.

"Hello?" I sputtered.

"Elsie? Is that you?" It was Carla from the Times.

"Yes, it's me."

"Listen up. I have an assignment for you. I'd like you to cover the Robson case from here on. Interested?"

"Sure." I already had more than a passing interest in Robson. In fact, I'd nearly passed out when I found him ripped to shreds. I could still see his hideous death mask. What fearful thing had he seen just before he died?

"I'll fax you what we have so far."

Carla Meeks is a nice woman, but her surname is a misnomer. There's nothing meek about her. Determined to snag the coveted executive editor slot, she had acquired in the bargain the undeserved reputation of a lipstick-wearing barracuda from envious co-workers, most of them men. I'd heard Carla called the "B" word more than once behind her back, and I don't mean "barracuda."

"Same rate as usual?" I said.

"If that's perfectly agreeable."

"Perfectly."

"Thanks, Elsie. I'll also fax you the assignment sheet. Call if you have any questions."

"Will do."

I had interviews to arrange and writing to do and...oh, no! I forgot about Skip coming to dinner. Why did my life always seem to go like this? I moved up here to Tahoe to get away from the stresses of city life. Sometimes it seemed like I had brought them all with me. I would have to throw the chili on the stove to cook and order that truckload of onions I promised him. Killer chili needed to simmer for half a day, but duty called. Tonight Skip would have to settle for a flesh wound.

By the time the doorbell rang, I was tweaking the

text on the draft of my article. I still couldn't come up with a good headline hook.

"Skip, come on in. I'm just finishing up something on the computer."

"Go ahead and finish. I'll make myself comfortable."

"I'll only be a minute. Go say hi to Cruiser. I told him you were coming. He's been beside himself all day."

"Yeah, I'll bet."

He hung his jacket on the hall tree and plopped down on the couch next to Cruiser.

"Hi ya, Cruiser, old buddy!" he said and gave Cruiser a friendly slap on the rump.

Cruiser grunted. He's never been one to go overboard. The only person I ever saw him run to greet at the door was Tom. Still, he wasn't above showing some sign of affection to those he really liked, and Skip definitely qualified. Cruiser thumped his tail on the couch once or twice, then rested a paw on Skip's leg. He stroked Cruiser's head to show his appreciation for the grand display of attention he was getting.

"Would you care for a glass of wine before dinner?" I stalled for more time so the chili could simmer longer. Another half-hour should do it, I figured. Mustn't disappoint. After all, my chili had a reputation to live up to.

"Sure. Although, I think I could drink the whole bottle tonight. It's been a rough week at work."

"So I hear. Red okay?"

"No white?"

"Sorry, it's all I have, other than beer."

"I'll take the beer, then. I've seen enough red lately."

Skip seemed on edge, and it wasn't just Robson's death that was bugging him; it was something else. From what he'd said earlier in the restaurant, I figured he needed to talk, and I knew a cold draft might help de-stress him and loosen his lips a little.

"Here, help yourself, Skip," I said, tossing him a six-pack. I always kept one in the fridge in case he dropped by. "I just have to check on the chili."

"Thanks." He tore one off and downed it like a pilgrim thirsting in the desert.

When I returned from the kitchen, Skip looked more relaxed.

"Feeling a little better now?"

"Yeah. Lots. I tell you, Beanie. These past 48 hours have been the absolute worst of my life. I've never seen anything like what I saw yesterday. It took my breath away."

"I know. I was there, remember?"

"Oh, yeah." Skip downed the last of his can of beer. "I think this discovery has a lot of people shook up."

"I know. It's got me rattled, too. It's more than that, though."

"Oh?"

Skip popped open another can, heaving a sigh in chorus with the hiss of the pop-top. "To add to everything else, I may lose my job."

"What?" I couldn't believe what I was hearing. Even if they teased him mercilessly, everyone knew Skip to be one of the best officers on the force. "Why? Surely not because of one silly remark a reporter quoted."

"No. Downsizing."

"Ah, yes. Downsizing. I've been hearing that word a lot lately." Even if free-lance pay was sporadic, I was thankful to be my own boss.

"You're not the only one. They're talking about layoffs in the department, starting with me, apparently."

"But why would they fire one of their best officers? Who are they going to use to hunt down criminals if you leave? Cruiser?"

The mention of his name jarred Cruiser from his slumber momentarily, then he resumed his imaginary rabbit chase.

"Don't even think that word, Beanie."

"What word?"

"'Fire.' Maybe if we don't say it, it won't happen."

"Have they told you for sure they're letting you go?" I was careful not to use *that word* again.

"No."

"Then you don't have anything to worry about. At least, not yet."

"Stoddard hates my guts. Always has, ever since he was my FTO at the academy."

"FTO?"

"Field Training Officer."

"Acronyms. How I hate them."

"Anyway, as I was saying..."

"Sorry, Skip."

"He made my life miserable, especially after I nearly shot my foot off."

"Isn't he the one who gave you that silly nickname?"

"Yeah. I thought he never would recommend me for duty. The jackass has just been waiting for a chance to get rid of me. I've always been a burr under his saddle blanket."

"But you've solved a lot of cases for him."

"That's why he hates me so much. He thinks I try to show him up, and he wouldn't want competition, especially now."

"What do you mean?"

"Haven't you heard? Stoddard's thrown his hat in the ring for the mayor's race."

"Oh, yeah. I saw one of his campaign posters the other day. Hitting the campaign trail kind of early isn't he? The Primary's still months away."

"He's determined to win. He wants to have his face firmly imprinted in people's minds by election day. I overheard him talking to someone on the phone about a speech he's giving in front of SaveNSense Supermarket."

"Why there?"

"It's a promotional thing. They're giving away a turkey to every registered voter who shows up. Free turkeys to vote for a turkey. Perfect. I'll lose my job, and Stoddard will be Tahoe's next mayor."

"Relax. He still has to beat out Thor Petersen first. Thor's a strong contender, and the environmentalists will back him. So will the Washoe; Sonseah Little Feather will see to that. Besides, you're a good cop, and Stoddard needs some reliable backup with a killer on the loose. Maybe he could learn a thing or two from you, especially if he has a yen for the mayor's hat."

"You can't teach an old dog new tricks, Beanie."

"Well, now. I wouldn't say that." I glanced at my old dog who at the moment wasn't doing any tricks, old or new. "On the other hand..."

"Even if he doesn't get elected, Stoddard plans to retire soon, and he just wants to coast to the finish line, you know? He isn't about to buck the system for my sake."

"Mm, hm. I know the type."

"Maybe I need to retire, too. They wouldn't be planning to cut me loose if I were doing a good job."

"Balderdash! You do a fine job, Skip. And don't let anyone tell you different."

"Thanks for the vote of confidence."

"Just stating a fact, my friend. If Stoddard's too stupid to see it, then it's his problem."

"Wrong. It's my problem." He set down his beer and blinked away pools of water at the corners of his eyes. I had never seen Skip cry before, not even at Tom's funeral. "I have a favor to ask you."

"Anything. Just name it."

"I need you to help me crack this case."

"How can I help?"

"It's my guess the Times will probably have you cover this, especially since you're the one who found the victim."

"You guessed right. It so happens I got a call from my editor just before you came over."

"Good. Nose around, like you're so good at."

"Gee, thanks a bunch!"

"You know what I mean. This is the biggest thing ever to hit Tahoe. If I can find out who wasted Robson, I can write my own ticket from now on. But if I can't hack it on this one, I'm history around here. Stoddard'll personally autograph my pink slip."

"You're not going anywhere if I can help it. Besides, maybe you can help me, too, on this assignment. I'll scratch your back, you scratch mine...and then we'll both scratch Cruiser's." We laughed as I gave Cruiser a vigorous tummy rub and his hind legs paddled the air in pleasure.

Skip lifted his beer can in a toast. "It's just you and me, Kid."

I toasted him with my glass of wine. "You, me, and Scoop Doggy Dog. Let's go eat some killer chili, with a truckload of onions. I hope you brought some Pepto Bismol."

Chapter Six

Late Tuesday Christmassy Cruiser, ornamented in his basselope antlers with dangling silver bells, sat beside me on the couch. I stroked his fur, intermittently glancing out the front window for any sign of Nona's red Volkswagen Beetle. Snow dusted the driveway like confectioner's sugar. The snowfall would be much heavier on the summit. I began to worry.

I lunged for the phone when it rang.

"Nona?" The urgency in my voice brought Cruiser to his feet. He shook his jowls, dislodging his jingling antlers and showering me with slobber.

"Hi, Mom!"

"It's late. Where are you?"

"It was snowing on the summit. The traffic was crawling at a snail's pace."

"Did you have to put on chains?"

"No, I managed to squeak through. Good thing, 'cause I didn't bring any along. Medwyn and I just finished dinner. We should be there in about five minutes."

I sighed with relief. "About time. Cruiser's getting impatient."

"Very funny, Mother."

The phone line clicked. It could only mean one thing. Soon, Medwyn Abercarn would be at the door demanding entry. Run for the hills, Cruiser!

I glanced around the living room. Everything seemed in order. Nervously, I fluffed the already-fluffed pillows. I added two more logs to the roaring fire. For the hundredth time, I straightened the magazines on the coffee table. COFFEE! I hadn't made any coffee. I had planned to have it ready before they arrived. Too late. I heard a knock at the door. They were already here! I repositioned Cruiser's cock-eyed antlers and went to admit my guests.

When I opened the door, standing beside a younger, slimmer version of me was Adonis in the flesh. Tall, muscular and tanned, Medwyn flashed a toothy smile no doubt intended to melt a skeptical mother's cold heart. The only thing missing was a bouquet and a box of See's Candies. He wore his shoulder-length, brownish blonde hair slicked back in a ponytail, but nothing seemed to be pierced, not even an earlobe.

"Mom! I'm so glad to see you." Nona hugged me as though to break me in two. It felt good to have her safe in my arms.

"I'm glad to see you, too, honey." Mother and child reunion aside, I focused on the young man.

"Mom, I'd like you to meet Medwyn Abercarn. Medwyn, this is my mother, Elsie MacBean."

"Nice to meet you, Medwyn," I said, offering my hand.

"Delighted to finally meet you, Ms. MacBean," Medwyn said, shaking my hand. His fools-gold hazel eyes locked with mine. "Nona's told me so much about you."

"Has she, now?" I felt mesmerized by his palpable charm and those strange eyes. He had an odd tick with his eyes, like the Felix the Cat clock I had when I was a kid. I'd lie in my bed in the dark watching its glowing eyes go back and forth, back and forth. Spooky.

"Yes. She talks about you constantly."

"Here, let me take your coats."

"Thank you, Ms. MacBean." He handed me his over-coat. I noticed the Armani label as I hung it in the closet. If clothes make the man, then Nona's taste in men had improv-ed.

"No need for formality. Just call me Elsie."

"Elsie it is, then."

"Everything looks so festive, Mom. I see someone's been busy decking the halls...and the dog."

We glanced in Cruiser's direction just as he shook his holiday headdress loose again. The silly felt antlers slid around his neck and hung upside down under his chin, creating a more comical effect than before.

"Yep. It only took me two hours to untangle the twinkle lights this year. I broke last year's record." Cruiser seemed grateful when I finally removed his antlers. "Would either of you care for some coffee?"

Medwyn nodded.

"Make it two," agreed Nona. "It was freezing out there. I need thawing out."

I brushed back a few strands of long, chestnut hair from my daughter's face, as my mother used to do for her daughter. Nona's spice-colored eyes grew warm as fresh gingerbread when she smiled at me. I gave her a peck on the cheek and patted her affectionately on her skinny model's behind, scooting her toward the living room.

"Go warm yourselves by the fire while I brew some java."

"Come on, Medwyn," Nona said. "Let's sit on the couch."

I saw him glance at Cruiser, the Sultan of Snooze, sprawled belly up in the middle of the couch. "Never mind. I'll sit here in this chair."

I scooped some Colombian beans into my Braun coffeemaker and grinder combo, Nona's gift to me last Christmas. She convinced me to junk the Mr. Coffee and Folger's crystals and join the ranks of the grinder groupies. I strained to hear the conversation from the next room, but the grinder drowned it out. Darn! I would never have had any problem eavesdropping with soft-spoken Mr. Coffee. But I could hear the familiar jangle of the metal tags on Cruiser's collar above the din. In a moment or two he ambled into the kitchen and lapped water from his bowl, splashing much more on the floor than he swallowed. Looking up to see if I was handing out any bedtime treats, he watched me intently for a few minutes as I prepared the coffee. When he saw no biscuits forthcoming, he U-turned for the living room.

Not five minutes later, I heard a terrible commotion. Nona dashed into the kitchen, a panic-stricken look on her face.

"Mom, come quick!"

"What's the matter?"

"Cruiser bit Medwyn!"

"Huh?" When I followed Nona into the living room, Medwyn didn't look any worse for wear, but his face was a thundercloud.

"Are you all right?" I asked.

"I suppose so."

"Here, let me see, Medwyn," Nona said, examining his hand. "I don't know what got into Cruiser. I've never seen him act that way before."

"You should have warned me your dog is vicious."

"He's not!" I said. "He's *never* bitten anyone in his whole life."

"You mean until now." Medwyn wiggled each of his digits as though he were counting them.

Cruiser wouldn't bite a flea. Well, maybe a flea, but I'd seen small children tug on his ears and ride him like a hobby horse with never a complaint from my gentle boy.

"It doesn't look like the skin's broken," Nona said.

"He's had all his shots, anyway," I added.

"I'll have my physician take a look at it tomorrow," Medwyn said. "He'll advise me what I should do."

"I'll shut Cruiser in the bedroom. I'm terribly sorry about this."

"No big deal. Let's forget about it, shall we?"

Nona and I shot a glance at each other. I knew she thought the same thing I did. For something that was "no big deal," it sounded like he might be planning to make a big deal of it. Maybe *this* was how he afforded Armani.

Ordinarily, Cruiser complained about being shut up in the bedroom, but he seemed glad to be far away from my guest.

"Nona, come and help me pour the coffee, will you?"

"Sure." She tailed me into the kitchen.

"Sorry about your date, Nona. I never dreamed Cruiser would bite *anyone*."

"It's all right. Meddy's just not the doggy type, I guess."

"You really haven't told me much about 'Meddy.' Like how does he afford designer clothes?"

"Well, I didn't want to tell you this, but he's the head of an international drug cartel."

"What?"

Nona smiled. "Relax, Mom. I'm just kidding. He works with the Tallis Corporation. They have a big project in the works."

"Tallis?" I retorted as though Nona had just said a dirty word.

"He mentioned something about a new resort they're building."

"You mean Cave Rock Resort?"

"Beats me. When Medwyn and I are together we don't talk much about work."

I felt my mercury rising. Finally, I could no longer contain myself.

"Oh, Nona. When are you going to find Mr. Right and settle down?"

"Really, Mother," Nona flared. "I don't think there is such a person as Mr. Right. Besides, I'm not ready to settle down, yet."

"Well, a girl your age should at least be thinking about it."

"I'm only 23. There's still plenty of time before I check into Happy Homestead Cemetery. Let's not get started on this subject again. Please?"

"I just don't want to see you make another mistake."

Nona took a deep breath; I knew she was about to let me have it with both barrels. "Mom, when are you ever going to stop treating me like I'm still in Pampers?"

"I didn't know I did."

"You're always trying to protect me from everything."

"I'm your mother. Isn't that my job?"

"No! Just be my mother and friend, not my jailer."

"We've always been friends, haven't we, Nona?"

"Yes, we have. And that's how I want it to stay. But you need to let me make my own mistakes, even if it means I don't always date who you want me to, or marry someone you haven't handpicked for me. I'm not your little girl any more, in case you never noticed. I haven't been for a long time."

Tears stung my eyes, but with every ounce of my will, I held them back. I knew they would serve no purpose. Nona was right. She wasn't my little girl anymore, but that didn't mean it hadn't stung like a swarm of African bees to hear her say it.

"I just thought you'd want to know a little more about someone you're dating, especially if you're getting serious."

"Who says I'm getting serious?"

"Well, aren't you?" I fished, but the line came up empty.

"It's too soon to tell. Give me a break, Mom. We only just started seeing each other. You wouldn't want me to rush into anything, would you?"

My visions of grandchildren toddling to greet me dissolved like snowflakes on my driveway. Then I thought of the incident moments before with Medwyn and Cruiser, and I knew the answer to her question.

"No, I don't want you to rush into anything, honey."

When Nona and I returned with the coffee, Medwyn was reading the front page of the Times. When he saw us, he tossed it back down on the coffee table and forced a smile. Nona sat down next to Medwyn and picked up the paper. I saw the color drain from her face when she saw the headline about Robson.

"Mom, why didn't you tell me about this before?"

"I thought if I did, you wouldn't come."

"You'd have been right. This is awful!"

"Nona tells me you're a reporter, Elsie," Medwyn said.

"Just a stringer for the Tahoe Times and a couple of other publications."

"She's just being modest, Medwyn. Mom's got quite a fine reputation as a writer." Nona bragging about her mother? Now there's a red herring if I ever smelled one.

"Are you covering the Robson case?" he asked.

"Yes."

"Any leads?"

"Not yet."

"Interesting case."

"I don't know if I'd say that, considering..."

"Considering what?" Nona asked.

"Oh, never mind." I didn't want to go into detail about what Cruiser and I had found out on the trail.

"Medwyn, Nona says you work for Tallis. What do you do there?"

"I'm in corporate liaison."

"What does that entail?"

"At the moment, handling certain details related to the Cave Rock Project."

"Like what, for instance?"

"What specifically is it you want to know, Ms. MacBean?" We were suddenly back to using last names.

"Really, Mom. Do you have to cross-examine Medwyn, for Heaven's sake?"

"It's okay, Nona," Medwyn said. "I don't mind. Being a reporter, I'm sure your mother's the curious type."

Curious was a nicer word than nosy.

"I have a feeling the Washoe aren't going to stand for this," I continued. "Not without a fight."

"You're probably right, but I don't think they have much chance of stopping it, unfortunately."

"That remains to be seen."

"Mother, please. Could you conduct this interrogation some other time?"

"It's late," Medwyn said. "I really should be leaving, anyhow. If you'll just retrieve my coat, I'll be on my way."

"Certainly." *Then I'll be happy to "fetch" you a cab.* I bolted for the Armani in the closet. "Sorry you have to leave so soon," I lied, as I offered him his coat and opened the front door. My heart sank when I saw the trail was piled high with snow, with a lot more coming down.

"We'll never make it back in this, Medwyn," Nona said. "Not in my car."

"We should have taken my Range Rover," Medwyn said.

"You can use the Jeep, Nona," I offered.

"Would it be all right if Medwyn stays the night?" She looked at me the same way she did when she begged me to let her have her first slumber party in grade school, except that one wasn't coed.

"Well..."

"Thanks, Mom."

"I'll prepare the guest room for him. You can use

the sleeper sofa in my office." I still felt guilty about Cruiser's unusual behavior and hoped this guy wasn't sue-happy. Maybe I could smooth his feathers by offering him a stay at Beanie's Bed and Breakfast.

Medwyn probably thought I didn't notice him smirking as I shut the door on the storm and re-hung his overcoat in the closet.

Chapter Seven

The morning sunlight streamed through my bedroom window. I pushed Cruiser aside, slipped into my comfy chenille robe and made tracks for the bathroom. I peeked into my office and saw Nona still counting Z's on the sleeper sofa.

The bathroom door was locked. I could hear the shower running, so I went to make some coffee while I waited for my turn. A quick cup of coffee, and it would be off with Medwyn and on with the skis.

With Medwyn behind locked doors, I figured I'd better let Cruiser out to piddle and sniff. If Medwyn didn't leave soon, I might end up biting him, too.

It must have snowed most of the night, because a good two feet of snow covered the ground. Perfect. Nona and I could go skiing, just as soon as I got rid of this butt-in-ski, Medwyn.

The past few winters a good snowfall sometimes hadn't appeared until February. Bad news for skiers and ski resort owners. Looked like that might be about to change. Tallis wouldn't be happy about it, though. The early snowfall would slow construction on Cave Rock Resort.

I watched with amusement as Cruiser sank to his chest in snow, trying to reach the nearest tree. He looked terribly annoyed with the whole business. In a moment, he was scratching at the back door to come back inside.

"Well, you broke the land speed piddling record, old buddy. Are you sure you took care of everything?"

He panted happily as he planted himself in front of his food bowl. His doggy smile drooped when he saw me shovel two cups of diet kibble into the bowl.

"Sorry, boy. Doctor's orders." He seemed to understand and began to eat his diet kibble somewhat more enthusiastically than he had so far. "Good Cruiser," I praised, patting his head.

"Good morning, Elsie." I jerked up and turned to face a clean-shaven, shiny-faced Medwyn, flashing me his glistening smile. The sun highlighting the gold in his hair and eyes made him look like an overgrown cherub. I expected him to sprout wings any moment and fly away. If wishes were horses...

"Morning. Sleep well?"

"Fine, thank you." He spotted Cruiser scarfing down his breakfast and gave him a wide berth. Cruiser did an about-face and walked a wide circle around Medwyn, growling as he left the kitchen. I felt like growling, too.

"Is Nona up, yet?"

"Yes, I think so."

"Would you care for a cup of coffee before you leave?"

"Please."

"It's already brewed. Help yourself. I'm going to get changed. Nona and I are going skiing this morning." If that wasn't enough of a hint for him to hit the road, I could hint a little harder next time.

He looked annoyed that he had to pour his own coffee. Unfortunately, I'd forgotten to wear my checkered apron. Maybe Rita would loan me hers. This guy was really starting to grate on my nerves. Nona and I would have to have a long conversation about Medwyn, and soon.

"'Morning, Mom. Is...'"

"He's in the kitchen. Go entertain him, will you? And for Heaven's sake, keep Cruiser away from him."

"Medwyn told me he's been bitten by a dog before."

"No big surprise to me. Just keep them apart until he leaves, okay?"

"I'll take him out for a walk."

"The snow is too deep for Cruiser to walk in."

"I meant Medwyn."

"Oh. Well, better take the leash, anyway."

"Ha, ha. Very funny. You don't like Medwyn much, do you, Mom?"

"I'm claiming the Fifth Amendment, honey."

"Give him a chance. You've only just met him."

What Nona didn't realize was that Medwyn had already decided he didn't like me, either. And he sure didn't like my dog.

"Care for any more coffee, Medwyn?" I asked.

"No thanks, Elsie."

I began to regret having told him to address me by my first name. I was glad I hadn't invited him to call me Beanie. I reserved my nickname for friends. By no stretch of the imagination would this guy ever be a friend of mine.

"My, look at the time," I said, glancing at my Swiss Army watch. "Time to hit the trails, Nona." I hoped Medwyn would make like a tree and leave.

"I'd best be going, too," Medwyn announced, rising. It worked!

"Why don't you come along, Meddy?" Nona said.

My heart sank at the thought of our day together ruined.

"I really had better go, Nona," he said. "Wouldn't want to wear out my welcome."

I'm sure he heard my sigh of relief. Nona shot me a frosty look.

"I'll be glad to drive you home, but we'll have to use my mom's car."

"Don't bother, I'll call a cab," Medwyn said. "I'm sure the roads are plowed by now."

"The phone's right over there," I volunteered.

Nona's eyes slitted. "You don't mind if I borrow your car a few minutes, *do you*, Mom?"

"Go ahead, but don't be too long." I knew when I was beaten.

"Thanks," Medwyn said.

"Don't mention it." I cringed when I saw him steal a kiss from Nona on his way out the door.

"Back soon," Nona called, and the door clicked shut behind her and her boyfriend.

I felt deserted, ticked off, depressed, all rolled into one. Powerlessness makes you feel that way, and I seemed powerless to stop my daughter from dating this guy.

Chapter Eight

I knew Nona had returned when I heard the front door and then the guest bedroom door slam. We probably wouldn't be skiing, at least not today. She was mad at me, and Nona's a pouter, like her dad. We both needed time to cool off.

I was just as upset with her for putting me on the spot the way she had. What bugged me most was that this Medwyn character would be coming back for Thanksgiving dinner. Yep, I was serving a turkey for Thanksgiving, but it didn't have feathers and go gobble, gobble.

"Come on, Cruiser. We're goin' for a ride." Cruiser bounded out the front door, barking his excitement, until he landed on his belly in the ice cold snow with a *whump*. His fervor dampened, he padded the rest of the way to the car, giving each wet paw a catlike shake. I hefted his snow-soaked hindquarters onto the passenger seat, coating the upholstery in damp dog hair.

I turned the key Nona had left in the ignition. When the engine kicked over, I shifted the Cherokee into 4-wheel drive and snowplowed out of the driveway and down the street. It was slow going until we hit the main road where the plows had already carved their way through last night's snowfall, then smooth sailing from there on.

"Here we are, boy," I said as I pulled into the lot at Sheriff's Headquarters. "Want to go see Skipper?"

Cruiser's tail thumped in response. Dogs know who their friends are. They can see to your very core and instinctively know the stuff you're made of. I've always thought I must have been a dog in a previous life, because I've always been intuitive like that, but my intuition didn't prepare me for what Skip was about to tell me when I entered his office with a damp dog in tow. I heard some people behind us in the hall laughing at Cruiser. If you own a basset hound, you get used to folks giggling and pointing.

Skip set the phone receiver in its cradle and signaled for me to close the door.

"Beanie! You're timing is perfect. I just took a call about a possible homicide."

"What? Another one?"

"Yep."

"Who?"

"Jay Caruso."

"How?"

"Same as Robson, apparently. Boy, I can sure tell you're a reporter. I'll save you the trouble of asking 'when' and 'where.' They found the body early this morning up at his mansion near Heavenly."

"Isn't Caruso the Tallis exec involved in that huge land grab awhile back?"

"Yeah, I think he was."

"Tallis scored big. The only losers were the Washoe. It was a portion of their trust land Tallis acquired. Our people's territory shrinks a little more every year."

"I know. And it's a rotten shame, too."

"Mind if the K-9 Corps comes along for the ride?"

"Do I have a choice?"

"Now, Skip. You never know, you might need someone with a cold, wet nose to sniff out a clue or two."

"I thought that's why you were coming along."

"Har-de-har-har. Go get the patrol car, will you? I'll be waiting here with your rookie. I'd better call Carla at the Times and let her know what's afoot."

"All righty, Ms. Sherlock."

Five minutes later, Skip screeched the patrol car to a stop. I loaded Cruiser in the back seat and climbed aboard. "Better fasten your seat belt," Skip said. "We're going all the way to the top."

"Right. I'm ready."

"Just one more thing."

"What?"

"Will you please roll down a window? Your dog

smells like the inside of my locker."

"What do you expect a wet dog to smell like, a bed of roses?"

"If I do, then I guess I'm out of luck, cause this one stinks — big time." He rolled down the driver's side window and shifted into four-wheel drive. "Okay, you two. Sit down, shut up, and hang on."

The car skidded momentarily on the icy pavement, then the snow tires grabbed, and the G-force pressed us to the seats. The siren screamed its chilling warning. In one respect, Skip is like Barney Fife. He never misses an opportunity to blast the siren.

As we sped down Pioneer Trail and skidded right onto Ski Run Boulevard, I glanced in the rearview mirror. Cruiser hung his head out the window, ears and tongue flapping in the jet stream, having the time of his life. As for me, all I could do was, as Skip so eloquently put it, shut up and hang on.

The car sped past Heavenly Valley Ski Resort. The red tram full of eager skiers glided along the cable up the sheer face of the snow-dusted mountain. I watched the first schussboomers of the season shooting down Gun Barrel, the most challenging run at Heavenly. A broken leg my third time out on the downhill slopes convinced me to pursue the gentler and, for me, more spiritually satisfying sport of cross-country skiing.

When we drove onto the grounds of the estate, another patrol car and the coroner's meat wagon were already on the scene. Jay Caruso's palatial aerie perched on a precarious granite ledge at the summit of the peaks surrounding Heavenly Valley. It could give you a nosebleed. An eagle's-eye panorama of the lake and white-blanketed peaks could be enjoyed from the mansion's expansive deck, but Caruso would never enjoy it again.

We entered the bird's-eye maple doors of the house. The view through the floor-to-ceiling window in the foyer was to die for, but I don't think Caruso exactly had that in mind when he built this place on upscale Chimney Rock Road. How could he know his elaborate dream house would eventually become his coffin?

The flash from a camera lit up the far end of the

foyer. Blood smeared the polished granite floor.

"In here, Cassidy," called Stoddard from the adjoining room. We didn't need directions. A trail of red marked the way.

When I glanced into the elegant study, I saw more red. Caruso appeared to have been tossed about the room like a rag doll. He lay limp and torn several yards from the French doors that led to a veranda. The walls were spackled with blood. His throat had been slashed open, a grimace of terror on his ashen face. Just like Robson's.

Camera flashes went off like fireworks on the Fourth of July.

"I *said* no reporters, Cassidy. What's *she* doing here?" Stoddard snapped, gnawing his cigarette.

"Sorry, editor's orders, Sheriff," I said.

"Well, just try to stay out of the way, huh?"

"Sure thing."

"How long has he been dead, Chief?" Skip asked.

"About 24 hours," Stoddard said, cigarette bobbing between his lips. I couldn't help noticing his boots, which accentuated his size 13 feet. No wonder Skip called him Bigfoot behind his back.

"Closer to 48," corrected the coroner. "No rigor left in the body, see?" He lifted the victim's hand. The clenched fingers uncurled. "This guy had been visiting the gym pretty regularly from the looks of him. It would take much longer for rigor to leave the body in his case. Not much decomposition, either."

Stoddard and the coroner stepped into the foyer while the investigative team bagged and tagged.

"I never saw so much blood, Beanie," Skip said.

"It's a 'study in scarlet,' all right." I lifted up a corner of the tarp covering the deceased that hadn't quite covered a bloody print on the ivory Berber carpet. "Say, Skip, did Caruso own a dog?"

"Don't know. Why?"

"I'd bet Cruiser's last biscuit that these are canine prints."

Skip pulled the tarp up to reveal several more prints. He plucked a wad of fuzz from the carpet and examined it.

"What's that, Skip? Killer dust bunny?"

"Looks like fur to me."

"Dog?"

"Could be. A big one, too, from the size of these prints here. Wonder where it is?" Skip glanced furtively around the room.

"It looks like the body was dragged from the foyer into the study. Would his own dog do that?"

"Well, someone did."

"Or some*thing*." A chill telegraphed up my spine.

"This is one for the X-Files, Agent Scully." One thing I've always loved about Skip is his ability to keep his sense of humor, no matter what.

"I'd say you're right, Mulder," I quipped back. "So, you think this guy's own dog killed him?"

"No, I didn't say that. Probably attacked the killer, more likely."

"But if that's the case..." I paused to make a couple of notes. "Shoot, this pen's out of ink. Never fails. Got a pen?"

Skip handed me a Pilot gel from his shirt pocket.

When the pen tip touched the page, it was Electraglide in blue. "Hmm. Nice pen. I'll have to pick up a six-pack of these."

"Forget the pen, Hemingway, what were you saying?"

"Just that it seems like there should be more prints in the foyer if the dog chased the killer away."

"Maybe it went out the..."

"We're not on coffee break, Cassidy," Stoddard barked. "Let's get this wrapped up. I'm due to give a speech at 11:00."

"Right, Chief," Skip said.

"And somebody get out there and keep the lookie-loos at bay. Did anybody think to bring the crime scene tape?"

One gloved officer began peeling back the blood-soaked carpeting while another carefully cut away portions of the red-stained wallpaper with an Exacto knife. Skip busied himself searching for clues and dusting for latent prints.

I suddenly felt my stomach loop-the-loop. "Hey, Skip, I think I'll get some fresh air...and make some notes."

"Sure." He added, out of Stoddard's earshot, "Why don't you go see what you can find out from the neighbors." He didn't have to ask me twice.

"Right. I'm outa here!"

I don't remember how I got out of there, except my feet moved like in a Roadrunner cartoon. I shut the door to the house of horrors on Chimney Rock Road and went to check on Cruiser.

"Nice K-9 you have here," an elderly gent said, petting Cruiser's head through the open window of Skip's patrol car.

"Thanks."

"What's his name?"

"Cruiser."

He laughed. "That's original. But I thought the police use German Shepherds for crime busting."

"He's just along for the ride. You live around here, Sir?"

"Sure do. In that house over there. I was just heading out for a walk when I saw the crowd."

"Did you know Jay Caruso?"

"Not really. We were just neighbors."

"Have you lived here very long?"

"Quite a long time now. I've been retired for nearly 20 years." No surprise there. Tahoe is a Mecca for well-heeled retirees.

"Seen any unusual activity the last couple of days?"

"Unusual activity?"

"Around Caruso's place, I mean."

"Well, let me think..."

While I waited for his response, a heavy-set, sixtyish woman wearing purple Spandex stirrup pants insinuated herself between us. Right then and there, I decided, when I am old, I shall *not* wear purple. Of course, she probably thought the same thing about my pink plaid deerstalker.

"It's terrible, just terrible. Imagine, a murder right on our own street. It's terrible, just terrible," she babbled. "Are the police in there? Are they letting people go inside?"

Yeah, sure lady. The sideshow barker is charging admission at the door. People were just too much to take sometimes.

"The public aren't allowed inside, Ma'am."

"Are you with the police?" she sniped. "You don't look like a police officer."

"I'm a reporter for the Tahoe Times." I brandished my pen and pad. "Would you care to make a statement for the press?"

"Who, me?" She took a step back. "Oh, no. I'm just an innocent bystander. I don't want to get involved."

As I watched her waddle back down the driveway, I vowed to lay off the chocolate chip cookies. At last, I knew the truth: Ogden Nash's famous "Purple Cow" poem wasn't about lavender bovines at all but obese women in Spandex stirrup pants.

"Say, Miss. I just remembered something," the man said.

"Yes?"

"I did see something rather odd from my window a couple of nights ago."

"What, Sir?"

"Some kind of animal. It was big! Ran across the street from Caruso's place and disappeared into the forest."

"Are you sure?"

"Sure as God made little green worms in little green apples."

While I waited for Skip to come out of Caruso's house I surveyed the vicinity of the murder scene. All I saw was an eagle circling a nearby ridge.

Chapter Nine

"Testing. Testing. One, two, three, four." A young man spoke into the microphone on the platform in front of SaveNSense.

"This is a pretty good turnout," Skip said, scratching his chin as he scanned the crowd in the snowy parking lot.

"Yeah, good turnout," I parroted, still thinking of the crime scene carnage.

"Only catch is they have to listen to Stoddard's speech before they get their free turkey. I hope Thor Petersen gives Stoddard a run for his money in this election."

"He will if looks count for anything, but Stoddard doesn't seem too worried about the competition."

"Probably because the turkey's too busy primping his feathers for his big appearance. He insisted we attend."

"Why?" I said.

"Riot control."

"Is he expecting trouble?"

"Don't know. I think he just wants us to keep all his adoring fans from rushing the stage for his autograph."

"Skip, *you're* a riot!" I laughed.

SCALE THE PEAKS FOR PROGRESS— STODDARD FOR MAYOR read the banner above the Sheriff's balding pate as he ascended the podium. The crowd clapped as he approached the lectern.

"Ever seen the Dilbert comic strip, Beanie?" muttered Skip.

"Yeah. He's a dead ringer for Dilbert's Tweedle-Dum boss."

We were still snickering when a hush fell over the crowd. Stoddard adjusted the microphone and pressed his lips to it as though he were about to French kiss the thing.

"Thank you..." Eeeeee. The mike screeched in protest. Everyone cringed as though he had dragged a garden rake across a blackboard. He moved back slightly then began again.

"Uh, thank you, Ladies and Gentlemen. I am pleased that so many of you could come today."

"Doesn't the putz know these guys are here for a free turkey?" Skip said, nudging me with his elbow. I stifled a giggle.

"What has made South Tahoe what it is today?" Stoddard paused, surveying the crowd, the drama lost on those impatiently awaiting their free gobblers. After shuffling through his notes for a moment, he finally answered his own question.

"The word on this banner above my head: Progress. That's progress with a capital P."

"Well, duh. We already know how to spell," Skip muttered.

I became aware of a commotion off to my right. Heads turned in the crowd. Then I saw banners and placards bobbing above the sea of heads: **Give Tahoe Back to the Washoe**; **Scrap the Cave Rock Project; Tread Softly on Mother Earth.** I didn't have to guess who would be the leader of the pack. Stoddard's jaw dropped. He stopped dead in the middle of his speech when Sonseah Little Feather and Dan Silvernail emerged from the crowd with thirty or so of the militant tribal faction, some beating ceremonial drums or shaking rattles while chanting and singing. Sonseah step-hopped to hypnotic native rhythms, the long white fringe of her beaded buckskin dress swaying gracefully as she danced. She looked noble and, I had to admit, beautiful.

I saw Stoddard nod to a couple of his deputies, who formed a human barricade between him and the demonstrators. He waited for their chanting to subside, then cleared his throat and continued speaking. "Progress first brought civilized people to this basin; it's progress that will keep them coming."

"Is this a *good* thing?" Sonseah shouted. The placards bobbed again in protest as the group cheered her words. I noticed a well-dressed man giving them a dirty look. Several other GQ types flanked him.

"Psst, Skip. Who are the suits?"

"Huh?"

"Those guys over there. Who are they?"

"I think they're with Tallis."

"This should get interesting." Stoddard drowned out my last comment.

"...and when I am elected, you will see a Tahoe like you've never seen before. It's progress that will make it happen. And with progress will come a cornucopia of prosperity for one and all. On election day, cast a vote for progress. Vote for Mike Stoddard for Mayor. Thank you for your support, and a big thank you to George Jenkins, Manager of SaveNSense."

Jenkins stepped up to the mike. "How about a round of applause for Sheriff Stoddard? And don't forget to pick up your free turkeys, folks." The spectators applauded briefly then milled around the table where the gobbler giveaway commenced.

When Sonseah and Dan began to march around the parking lot, a man stepped from among the bystanders and yanked Sonseah's sign from her hand, ripped it up, and threw it to the ground.

"Filthy Injuns! Go back to the reservation where you belong," he shouted and spat in Sonseah's face. Dan hit him over the head with his placard, more angry words were exchanged, then fists began flying. Others joined in the melee, including one or two Tallis suits.

Several deputies, including Skip, stepped in to break it up. Soon, things had calmed down. Dan picked up his Stetson from the pavement, brushed it off and placed it back on his head. Gradually the demonstrators dispersed.

"Whew!" Skip said. "Talk about a turkey shoot. What's next?"

"It's anyone's guess."

"I'd better make tracks. I'll see you later, Beanie."

"Yeah, I gotta go, too. I have a big turkey to stuff tomorrow."

"But I thought you don't eat meat."

"I meant my daughter's boyfriend."

Skip grinned. "You really don't like him, do you?"

"How'd you guess?"

"Listen. Here's what you do. If he gives you any trouble, just sic that killer basset of yours on 'im."

"I already tried that."

Chapter Ten

After returning from Stoddard's campaign speech, I sat for an hour in front of the computer, staring at the white field on the screen and the blinking cursor. My fingers were poised over the keys, but the words just wouldn't come. I suffered from a serious case of writer's block. Too many things were bugging me. With the likes of Medwyn dating my daughter and what I'd seen up on Chimney Rock Road earlier, who wouldn't be distracted? I was also disturbed by the mayor wannabe's environmental agenda, not to mention the ugly culture clash I had witnessed earlier at Stoddard's speech. If we were lucky, this growing dispute over Cave Rock wouldn't end up in all-out war. If things kept up this way, who knew? Sonseah and Dan were stirring up the hornet's nest, and they weren't about to back down. Compromise wasn't in their vocabulary. Perhaps I would be able to talk some sense into them at the next Tribal Council meeting. On the other hand, I worried about what might happen to Washoe country if Stoddard were actually elected. I wondered if I shouldn't have joined in the demonstration earlier. Maybe I should be rounding up votes for Thor.

As I stared out the window Thanksgiving day, peeling onions for the stuffing, I still couldn't get the crime scene out of my mind.

"What's wrong, Mom?" Nona asked. "You seem like you're on another planet this afternoon."

"So what else is new?"

"Sorry about yesterday."

"All forgotten."

Nona planted a kiss on my check. "Me, too."

I tossed her an onion. "Here, grab a knife and start

dicing. Say, I thought Medwyn was going to help us prepare dinner. Where is he, anyway?"

"He'll be here soon. He's not much good in the kitchen."

"So I've noticed."

"Give him a break. After all, he's a man, isn't he?"

"That's no excuse. You've got to break them in early, honey, or it's a lost cause. They'll turn you into a serving wench, if you give them half a chance."

"But Pop wasn't like that."

"Because I trained him right."

"You didn't use a choke collar, did you?"

"Nah. Just treats from Cruiser's yum-yum nook."

We laughed so hard tears ran down our cheeks, or maybe it was the onions. Just then the doorbell rang.

"Oh, it must be Medwyn," Nona said, dashing for the door with Cruiser hot on her heels.

I continued peeling. I wished I could peel out of the house and leave Nona to entertain her guest.

"Am I missing something funny in here?" Medwyn stood at the kitchen door. Too late to make my escape.

"Mom, look what Medwyn brought for you."

Medwyn handed me a bouquet.

"Daisies." *What, no See's Candy?* "My, how thoughtful of you, Medwyn. But you really shouldn't have."

"Well, we got off on the wrong foot before. I'd like us to be friends, Elsie. A nice lady like you deserves flowers."

"Yes," Nona said. "Especially when she's making such a yum-yummy dinner, huh, Mom?"

I looked at Nona. She winked at me, and we burst out laughing. Medwyn looked puzzled and went to make himself comfortable in my Tom's easy chair.

The clock on the mantle chimed five.

"Soup's on!" I hollered. When I heard the familiar sound of the evening newspaper rustling, I half expected to see Tom enter the kitchen door, but instead Medwyn appeared and took a seat at the head of the table.

"Shall I carve?" he asked.

"Carve what?" I said.

"The turkey, of course."

"If you can find one here on the table, go ahead and carve it."

Medwyn surveyed the various dishes set before him: tofu "turkey" loaf; golden yams; Brussels sprouts; Waldorf salad; celery and carrots; and sage, acorn, and onion stuffing. There wasn't a gobbler in sight. I watched with wicked amusement as the realization sunk into Mr. Abercarn's brain that he was about to have his first meatless Thanksgiving feast.

After a moment or two he finally found his tongue. "No turkey?"

"I'm sorry, Medwyn," Nona said. "I should have warned you before inviting you for dinner. Mom's a vegetarian."

"You mean you don't even have turkey on Thanksgiving? What's Thanksgiving without a turkey?"

"Why don't you ask a turkey sometime?" I said.

"Mom hasn't served turkey for years. To tell you the truth, I've never missed it. I always enjoyed Thanksgiving a lot more knowing nothing had to be killed to feed us."

Medwyn didn't say a word, but plopped down in his chair and busied himself unfolding his napkin. I thought for a moment he might burst into tears. I hoped this didn't mean he'd be asking for his daisies back, even though I knew they were a shameless bribe.

"Thanks again for the bouquet, Medwyn. It's the perfect touch for our holiday table."

"You're welcome."

"Does your family live here in Tahoe?" I asked.

"No, I live alone now." He didn't look up. He just kept herding Brussels sprouts around on the plate with his fork.

"Have you lost someone recently?"

"My mother died."

"You never told me, Medwyn," Nona said, laying her hand on his. "I'm so sorry."

"Me, too," I said. "How did it happen?"

Medwyn set down his fork, wiped his mouth and folded his paper napkin so painstakingly I thought he was making an Origami swan.

He finally set down the napkin and cleared his throat. "You know, I think I'm finished here. Will you please excuse me?"

"Certainly."

Medwyn rose from the table and went into the living room. I glanced over at Nona, who glared back at me. Her eyes were two flame-throwers. If I had served a turkey, Nona could have roasted it with one look. I stared at my own plate, herding Brussels sprouts.

As Nona and I ate the rest of our meal in gravy-thick silence, Cruiser watched the activity at the dinner table with his usual aplomb, assured that if he sat long enough wearing "the look," one of us would eventually take pity and slip him a tidbit. It had never failed before; why would it now? He watched every movement of the wrist, every nuance of fork and spoon, while feigning an air of detachment. I could hear the gears rotating wildly in his doggie brain as he plotted his avenue of attack. He honed in on Medwyn's abandoned plate of food. He moved in closer. A little closer. Still nothing. At last, the coup de théâtre. He pressed his chin on my knee, slopping up my last clean pair of slacks, and peered at me with Sad Sack eyes.

Napoleon himself couldn't have countered Cruiser's suppertime strategy. I had met my Waterloo. I conceded defeat and set Medwyn's plate down on the floor for Monsieur Cruiser Bone-aparte, knowing he wouldn't be interested in his diet kibble after this royal feast. I'd have to give him an extra long walk, and me, too. Maybe Nona's boyfriend hadn't enjoyed my cooking, but I had to let my belt out three notches after I finished eating.

Nona and I finally joined Medwyn in the living room to give our food some settling time. Cruiser skirted our dinner guest and curled in front of the fireplace to warm his backside. The fire flickered in the darkened room, casting strange shadows on the knotty pine walls. Power animals — bear, wolf, coyote, eagle — leapt and soared in the shifting, shimmering light from the fire.

I thought of the camping trips in Desolation Valley with Grandfather when I was his little "Papoose". I remembered the wonderful tales he told on summer nights when

I'd swear I could count every star in the heavens.
Grandfather's eyes sparkled in the light from the crackling
campfire as he wove with his gnarled, brown hands the leg-
end of how Lake Tahoe came to be. I can still hear him
speak in his voice as deep as the lake when he first told me
the story.

"Papoose, have I ever told you the tale of
Kanuwapi?"

"No, Grandfather."

Grandfather slowly lit his long pipe. The end of the
ceremonial pipe glowed in the darkness as his leathery cheeks
billowed with each puff. The white smoke transformed to
sacred spirits in the night air.

"Tell, Grandfather, tell!" I implored.

"Patience, Papoose."

At last Grandfather set his pipe down on a large, flat
rock near where he sat. As he spoke, wisps of tobacco smoke
blew through the gaps in his teeth like mist through a weath-
ered fence.

The crackling of logs in the fire sent a shower of
sparks up the chimney, jolting me from my reverie and
Cruiser from his after-dinner nap. He looked around momentarily, then stretched out full length in front of the fire.

"That's an interesting artifact above the mantle,"
Medwyn remarked, pointing to the bow displayed there.
"Washoe?"

"Yes, it belonged to my grandfather. He had no
grandsons, so I inherited it when he died. I have the hand-
made arrows and quiver, too." I knew it went against Washoe
custom to keep the belongings of the dead. It was usual to
destroy them at the time of burial, but I just couldn't part
with this last vestige of my Native American heritage.

"Can you shoot it?"

"Yes. I haven't practiced in a long time, though."

"You do hunt, then."

"No, of course not!"

"Oh, yes. Vegetarian."

"I'm strictly an acorn eater."

Medwyn's smile didn't quite reach his eyes.

Time for a little après dinner entertainment, I decided. "Hey, Nona," I said.

"What?"

"Did Grandpop ever tell you the story of Kanuwapi?"

"No, I don't think so."

"Want to hear it?"

Nona rolled her eyes. "Oh, Mom," she sighed. "Go ahead."

I leaned back comfortably in my chair, slipped off my shoes and tucked my feet up under me. "Kanuwapi was the bravest warrior of the Washoe tribe," I began. I could hear the echo of Grandfather's words as I spoke. It was almost as though he were speaking through me. "He wanted to marry the Chief's beautiful daughter, but the Chief would not allow the marriage until Kanuwapi performed a great deed that would be passed down to future generations.

"So Kanuwapi traveled far away to the North. He found a vast, snowy valley where lived a great, white bear, the largest one Kanuwapi had ever seen. Surely if he killed this bear, his deed would be great enough to win the hand of the Chief's daughter. But when he shot his arrows, they would not penetrate the bear's thick, white fur. Kanuwapi prayed to the Great Spirit, and the Spirit spoke to him in a dream to shoot an arrow into the bear's nostril.

"Kanuwapi's arrow missed its mark. The bear awoke and chased Kanuwapi. He ran as fast as he could, but the bear was closing in. The earth shook beneath the bear's weight, and his thunderous footsteps caused great landslides and avalanches."

Medwyn's eyes were glowing embers in the dark. Cruiser whined in his sleep, paddling the air in pursuit of whatever it is dogs chase in their sleep.

"Don't stop, Mom. What happened then?" Nona asked, her eyes wide with childlike excitement.

"Kanuwapi finally reached this valley. When the white bear came into the valley, Kanuwapi turned and shot his last arrow. The arrow shot straight into the bear's nostril, and he sank into the mud and died. Because he was a bear from the cold North, after he died great snowstorms filled the valley with snow, burying the great, white bear.

"When summer came, the snow melted and filled the valley with water, and the tribe called it 'Tahoe.' The Chief was well pleased with Kanuwapi's great deed, and

Kanuwapi married the Chief's daughter." I raised my hands above my head as Grandfather would have at the end of the story. "Wah-she-shue, edeh-weeh-deeh-geh-eeh — Da-ow-a-ga. This is the land of the Washoe people — Lake Tahoe."

The room was so silent, you could have heard a flea drop off of Cruiser's back and hit the floor. At this point, Grandfather would have lifted his pipe again to his lips, puffing smoke signals to mingle with the scent of pines in the crisp evening air.

Cruiser yelped when a spark flew out of the fireplace and singed his tail. We all jumped like we'd been shot with one of Grandfather's obsidian-tipped arrows.

"Great story, Mom!"

"Fascinating," Medwyn droned.

Cruiser groaned and licked his hurt pride.

Oh, well. At least I had one appreciative listener in my audience.

"Well, I hate to eat and run," Medwyn said, rising, "but I think I'd better be going."

I didn't argue the point.

"Thank you for the dinner. And story time."

"No problemo."

"She's got a million of 'em," Nona said.

"Good-bye, and thanks again," Medwyn said, more out of courtesy than sincerity.

"Ciao," I said.

"I'll see you out, Meddy," Nona said shutting the door behind her. The shutting of that door was symbolic to me at that moment; Nona seemed to be shutting me out of her life.

I peeked through the curtain as Nona followed Medwyn to his car. They talked for a few minutes. Then I saw him draw her close to him and kiss her. It was only moments, but the kiss seemed to last forever before he finally climbed into the car. As I watched him drive away, I hoped it would be the last I ever saw of Medwyn Abercarn. But I sensed I would be seeing a lot more of him, and a lot sooner, than I would like.

"Mom, I'll be back. I'm just going out for a few minutes."

"What for?"

"I thought I'd get some margarita mix for us."

"The grocery stores won't be open now."

"I'll go to a convenience store. They're always open."

"But the roads will be icy without chains, dear."

"Well, I was going to ask..."

"The keys are in my coat on the hall tree."

"Thanks," Nona said, fishing for the keys.

"Be careful, okay?"

"I will." The door closed. Cruiser and I were alone again. Margarita mix, my foot. How dumb did she think I was? I knew where she had gone, and it wasn't to the corner 7-11. I sure wasn't getting to spend much time alone with my daughter. In fact, so far, I'd spent none, thanks to Medwyn.

"Walkies, Cruiser?" I coaxed, brandishing his leash, but when I opened the back door, he spotted the generous layer of snow on the porch and retreated to the fireside and his pillow. Even the magic word wasn't going to persuade him to get his paws wet. I knew he didn't like the snow, but there was something else about Cruiser tonight I couldn't quite put my finger on. He had been acting peculiar all evening. At first I thought it was because there was a stranger in the house, and the stranger had made it plain he wasn't a dog lover. But there was something else. Perhaps he's sick, I thought. No, that wasn't it, either. If he were sick, he wouldn't have begged for food at the table. I finished up the dinner dishes, then sat down beside him on the sofa to read the paper and toast my toes by the fire. He shifted from his pillow and rested his head on my lap, as though seeking comfort. I stroked him as I read. Finally, we both nodded off. It had been a long, tiring day, at least for one of us.

Chapter Eleven

Car lights glared in my eyes. Cruiser's head snapped up when he heard the car door slam. I glanced at the mantle clock. Nearly Midnight. We both met Nona at the door.

"You've been gone a long time. Didn't have any trouble, did you?"

"No. I just went to see Medwyn."

"I see."

"No, I don't think you do."

"What you do with your boyfriend is no business of mine, Nona. You're a grown-up woman and able to make your own judgments."

"I don't need to make any judgments about Medwyn, Mother. You've already made them for me."

"What do you mean?"

"You've been so rude to him from the moment you met him. He was a guest in your home."

"Funny, I don't recall inviting him."

"Why don't you like Medwyn?"

"What's to like? For starters, I hate his name. What kind of a name is Medwyn Abercarn, anyway?"

"I think Shakespeare said it first, but "What's in a name?""

"I can just see it, Wenona Abercarn. What a hoot! Pop would do somersaults in his grave."

"For Heaven's sake, relax, Mom. I'm not marrying the guy."

"Not yet, you mean."

"This isn't just about names. I mean, he can't help what his parents named him. What is it, really?"

"You want to know what I don't like? I'll tell you what I don't like. This guy is pompous, cold, and conceited."

"Well," she huffed, hooking her hands on her hips. "That's not a bit judgmental, is it? Admit it, Mother. It's really about Tallis, isn't it?"

"I'm not going to lie to you. That's part of it. But mainly I don't want you to get too stuck on this guy, Nona. Trust me. He's all wrong for you."

"Why don't you let me decide that? You said I'm a grown-up woman. So let me be one, for crying out loud. You just don't want me to ever be happy, do you?" Nona's eyes were two shimmering pools.

"That's not true, and you know it."

Cruiser looked up at us as the pitch of our voices rose to a crescendo.

"Yes, it is," Nona ranted, her tears flowing freely. "The truth is, you can't stand being alone since Daddy died, so you want me to be your little girl forever. You'd have me still living here and ordering me in by ten o'clock, if you had your way. Well, in case you never noticed, I stopped being your little girl a long time ago, Mom. So get a life, already."

"How dare you talk to me that way? Did I teach you no respect for your elders?" I said, tears spilling down my own cheeks.

Cruiser placed himself like a furry referee between us. He pawed my leg and then Nona's, his brow furrowed with concern, wondering why we were making so much noise. He never allowed Tom and me to raise our voices, either. Seeing that we were upsetting Cruiser always quickly defused our anger. It worked now for Nona and me.

"Let's not argue," I said, wiping tears on my sleeve. "It's Thanksgiving. Let's not spoil it. You always loved Thanksgiving, especially when Pop was here."

Nona's brow smoothed.

"You're right. Let's not argue."

I stroked my daughter's satin hair, as my mother often did mine, then kissed away her tears. "Why don't I make us some fresh coffee?"

"Won't it keep you up all night?"

"It doesn't matter. I still have more writing to do tonight before I hit the hay. I could use a little java jive."

"Okay."

"Come and sit with me in the kitchen while I brew

some." I hugged her. "You know I love you, don't you, Nonie? I only want what's best for you, that's all."

"I know," she said, bumping her head against my shoulder, like she used to do as a little girl. Something tugged at my heart as though to rend it in two. Suddenly I hated myself for giving her a moment's unhappiness. We had been apart too long to spend our precious hours together quarreling, especially over the likes of Medwyn.

Nona sat at the kitchen table while the coffee finished perking. I set out two cups. I always used a special one for Nona when she came to visit. It had a beautiful hand-painted scene of two cross-country skiers traversing a snowy meadow, as we often did. I poured it to the brim with Java City blend, poured one for myself and sat down at the table with her to make peace. Our Indian ancestors would have smoked the ceremonial pipe, but we were both militant non-smokers, so a percolated powwow would have to suffice.

"I bought extra tickets to the Firemen's Ball this Saturday. I thought you might like to come along."

"That sounds great! Can I can bring a friend?"

"Of course. I can set you up with a date, if you like. I know a really nice guy at the Times who's been dying to meet you." It might just work, I thought.

"No need. I'm sure Medwyn will be glad to escort me. Is that going to be a problem?"

I sighed. I knew when I was beaten. "Bring anyone you like, Nona."

"Who are you going with?"

"Skip Cassidy."

"Oh, yes. The deputy. Are you and he seeing each other?" It was Nona's turn to be nosy.

"No. We're just good friends."

"Oh? How good?"

"That's none of your business, young lady."

"Shoe's on the other foot now, huh, Mom?"

I reached across the table and batted at her hand. "So, do you want to make it a foursome?"

"Sure. I don't have anything better to do."

"Gee, you sound just like your father. I hope you won't be too bored while you're here."

"Not if we do a little skiing, like you promised. Are

we going to go tomorrow?"

"If this snowstorm ever lets up."

"Yeah, it's been coming down pretty heavy. By the way, have you seen any wild animals hanging around here lately?"

"Not since your boyfriend left." A frown clouded her pretty face. "I was just kidding, honey."

"Oh, I know, Mom. It's not that."

"What's wrong, then?"

"I thought I saw something when I drove up to the cabin earlier."

"What did you see?"

"I...I'm not sure. I only got a glimpse, then it disappeared into the woods."

"Probably just a coyote. They get desperate for food this time of year. We lose a lot of cats around here, but not many basset hounds, thank goodness." Cruiser knew I was talking about my favorite boy and drummed his tail on the floor.

"Well, I suppose it could have been a coyote. Only, it looked a lot bigger."

"It couldn't have been a bear. They're all hibernating."

"Whatever it was, it was huge." I know it sounds impossible, but it looked something like a...a polar bear."

"You're right, Nona. That *is* impossible. Grandpop's story must have made quite an impression on you."

"Well, let's just hope it doesn't come around again."

"I'll be sure to cover the garbage cans tonight if bears are hanging around."

"Where are we going skiing tomorrow?" Nona asked.

"I thought maybe Spooner Lake." I suddenly had a distressing thought. "Medwyn doesn't ski, does he?"

"I don't know. I'll ask him when I see him tomorrow."

I should have kept my big mouth shut. "But you just saw him this evening, Nona. Your grandmother always said, 'Familiarity breeds contempt.'" She was certainly right about that adage, especially where Medwyn and I were concerned.

"I didn't see him."

"But earlier you said..."

"I know what I said. You never let me finish. I couldn't find his place."

"But I thought you knew where he lived."

"Not exactly, we always meet at a coffee shop or something."

"Are you sure you had the right address?"

"I think so. Maybe I just wrote it down wrong."

"Not his house, huh?"

"There *was* no house. It was a vacant lot."

Chapter Twelve

After Nona said good-night and went to bed, I read in the living room for awhile, then hacked at my computer until nearly two in the morning before e-mailing my latest article to Carla. Something about this case kept nagging at me. No wonder I couldn't sleep. Cruiser had given up on me hours earlier and made himself comfortable on my bed.

Outside, the storm gathered momentum until the pines no longer sighed but shrieked in the wind, or was it not the wind I heard but some beast wandering in the stand of trees that sheltered this seemingly secure abode? More than once I thought I heard something scraping against the outer walls of the cabin. Surely, it was just a bough whipped by the wintry gale that huffed down the chimney, stirring the dying embers of the fire to life again. Was something snuffling at the back door to capture the scent of potential prey within, or was it only gusts of wind blowing through imperceptible gaps in my log fortress that suddenly seemed vulnerable?

Exhausted, I reasoned my imagination was working overtime. I saved my work and shut down the computer. As I started to get up, I knocked the phone book on the floor and it fell open to the A's.

"Hmm. I wonder..."

I began thumbing through it looking for Medwyn's last name. AARON, ABBOT, ABEL, ABERCROMBIE...no ABERCARN. Unlisted, of course. Great, my daughter was dating her mother's worst nightmare, and I didn't even know where he lived. Just then, I heard a scraping sound outside my window. Well, maybe Medwyn wasn't my *worst* nightmare. I shut off the lights and scurried off to my bedroom. Like a frightened child, fearing a dreadful monster would lunge from somewhere in the darkness, I quickly shifted Cruiser out of my way, and leaped into the safety of my bed. I yanked the covers over my head, whispered a prayer, and soon, against my will, the moaning wind lulled me to sleep.

The next morning was clear but windy. Nona woke me early. Too early. I didn't mention the noises I'd heard. I figured she could tell I'd had a rough night by the bags under my eyes. I was still sandy-eyed and grumpy as we trudged through a four-foot snow base to load our skis and gear in the Jeep. Cruiser watched us from the window. Although he wanted to come along, he wouldn't like sinking up to his dewlaps in cold, white stuff. To my knowledge, they hadn't yet invented skis for dogs. He would have to be content to lounge around the house, a change from his usual life in the fast lane.

The guy I hired had already shoveled last night's snowfall from the driveway. The black dots of asphalt peeking through the ice reminded me of Domino, the Dalmatian that always rode with Tom in the fire engine. I shifted into reverse and backed down the driveway. I heard Cruiser's barks of protest as we drove away. He knew my weakness. It wasn't the first time he'd given me the "doggie in the window" routine. When I returned, he would probably ignore me for hours to punish me.

"Where are we going, Mom?" Nona asked when I steered onto the highway and headed in the opposite direction of our destination.

"I decided to go to Kiva Beach instead of Spooner Lake. It's quieter there this time of year."

"Near Valhalla?"

"Uh, huh. You remember when we went to the Gatsby Days celebration there last summer?"

"Yeah. I loved those period costumes everyone wore."

"And the quilting and art displays."

I could still hear the blacksmith, pounding out his metallic rhythms, which resonated through the grounds, enhancing the recreated ambiance of gentler days. In the evening, we attended a ball in rustic but grand Valhalla, the historic summer home that also serves as a popular setting for Tahoe society wedding receptions.

"Remember the trail we hiked along the lake?" Nona asked. "It would be great for skiing."

"You read my mind. It's even marked for cross-country."

"This is going to be great!" Seeing her shifting eagerly in her seat took me back twenty years to the time we drove up here to visit my parents.

Mom and Dad didn't get to see their granddaughter too often, but we did drive up occasionally for a visit. Whenever we did, my parents and I took Nona to the kiddie amusement park on Lake Tahoe Boulevard. She got so excited, she hopped up and down on the car seat, squealing, "Fairy wheel! Want to ride fairy wheel!"

She looked nearly as excited as then when I pulled off of Highway 89, traversed the bike trail crossing and meandered down the snowy avenue to our destination. Not a soul was in sight as we approached the deserted parking lot. No throngs of tourists converged on the Tallac Historical site. Tiny chipmunks skittered from tree to tree, startled by our presence in the silent forest.

We drove past the padlocked entrance to "Lucky" Baldwin's historic estate. His casino, which in the 1920's attracted wealthy patrons all the way from San Francisco to navigate precarious unpaved mountain roads in their fine touring cars, had long since been torn down. Often on warm summer days, Nona and I pedaled our bicycles down the bike trail to the site. We stopped to rest in the rustic gazebo beside the trout pond where Lucky's beautiful daughter, Dextra, once sipped lemonade and gazed out upon the pristine lake through the Tallac shore pines.

The first building on the grounds housed an exhibit devoted to the ancestry of our people. Visiting children, including my Nona, delighted in exploring huts typical of the Washoe that stood displayed in a clearing outside the building. Inside the museum, several beautifully woven Washoe baskets and other cultural artifacts were encased in glass cabinets. I was glad that my young daughter could appreciate the few remnants that remained of our heritage. Too often it seemed that she had little enough connection with her Native American roots.

Nona sealed the Velcro closures of her new Rossignol boots and snapped into her state-of-the-ski Kneissels as I finished lacing up my Frankenstein clunkers. I strapped myself into my Neolithic, bear-trap bindings and pulled the flaps of my deerstalker hat over my ears, fastening the tie under my chin. Easy to spot in her flashy, figure-hugging ski duds, Nona was already halfway to the trailhead before I had even stepped from the parking lot.

"Hey, speedy. Wait for me!" I yelled. She looked back, grinned and waved.

"Hurry up, slowpoke! Even Cruiser's faster than you are."

As I traced twin grooves on the path, I saw small animal tracks—snowshoe rabbit, deer, coyote—imprinted in the virgin snow, which sparkled like the glittered Christmas card Nona made for me in Kindergarten. A gust of wind loosened a heavy clump of snow from the pines, and I dodged as it thudded to the ground nearby. A woodpecker bobbed like a child's mechanical toy inch-by-inch down a nearby tree trunk, unconcerned by my presence as he repeatedly poked his sharp beak into the bark in his search for juicy grubs. The sun graced a sky as blue as a newborn baby's eyes. Angel wing clouds brushed the marshmallow peaks towering in the distance over the still, gray lake, looking so different than it had in July. A string of Canada geese glided in the water along the Tallac shore, glistening ribbons trailing in their wake on the lake's mirrored surface. Leading the group, the magnificent gander honked instructions to the feathered punters, his ancient calls hanging frozen in the rarefied air.

We skied along the trail beside the lake, occasionally pausing in the glistening woods to appreciate the silence. All I heard was the thudding of my own heart. Draped in shadows from the virgin grove of sugar pines, the white-sheeted fields imbued me with such a deep sense of peace and reverence, I felt tears flowing down my windburned cheeks. Or perhaps it was the strain of trying to keep up with Nona.

"Mom, how are you doing back there?" called Nona. "Wanna rest for a minute?"

"I could use a break."

We glided over to a sunny clearing and unclamped our skis. A fallen pine tree provided a comfortable bench for us to sit on while I tried to catch my breath.

"Hungry, Mom?"

"Starved, honey," I puffed. "What have you got?"

Nona dug into her backpack, then pulled out some leftover Waldorf salad and sage and onion stuffing, two bananas and a pair of energy bars. She arranged our banquet on the log between us.

"When did you pack all this?" I asked.

"This morning while you were still snoring away with old Rip van Wrinkle. You must have stayed up pretty late last night. I woke up at one o'clock, and you were still hacking at your computer."

"I didn't hit the sack until two. I don't know if it was the heavy dinner, the coffee, or the storm, but I had one heck of a restless night."

"That was quite a storm, all right. I didn't sleep much, either. I kept hearing things."

"What things?"

"Scraping, scuffling sounds. Just the pine trees whipping around outside, I suppose."

Neither of us said anything, but I knew what we were both thinking. A second alarm went off in my head, but again I ignored it. The sun shining brightly in the clearing scattered any shadows that threatened to spoil our outing. For the moment, not a worry was in sight.

We ate and rested for about half an hour before the sun slipped behind smudges of charcoal clouds enveloping the craggy peaks of Mount Tallac.

"We'd better head back," I said.

"I think you're right, Mom. Those clouds look like they mean business. Let's take the shortcut back."

"Okay by me," I said, surveying the darkening sky.

We paused a moment at the edge of the woods to enjoy one last vista of the mountains, looking more ominous than majestic in the shadow of the approaching storm. I heard the honking of the flock of geese overhead, startled to flight by the rumble of thunder. Urged onward by the speed with which the clouds gathered and concerned about possible lightning strikes, I skied faster toward the parking lot.

I was still trying to catch up with speed skier Nona when I heard her scream. I skied as fast as I could to where she stood, her face as pale as a sheet. For a moment, we both stood frozen in our tracks, unable to speak.

"N...Nona, did you bring your cellular?" I gasped for air like a beached trout, partly from overexertion, partly from the sight of what we'd happened upon.

"Y...yes," Nona sputtered back, handing me her phone.

I dialed Skip. There was no answer at first, then a familiar voice came on the line.

"Officer Cassidy."

"Skip. Thank God. It's me. Our killer has struck again."

"Where?"

"Kiva Beach."

"What are you doing down there?"

"Cross-country skiing. We're located about 100 yards west of the parking lot."

"Hang tight, Beanie. I'm on the way."

I handed Nona back her cellular. Her coloring went from white to green as she gawked at the contorted face and the terror-filled eyes trained toward a stand of sugar pines to our right. The snow surrounding the body looked like some-one had spilled a cherry snow cone. I would have passed Nona a barf bag if only I'd thought to pack one. Lip gloss? Check. Sunscreen? No problem. Barf bag? No way, at least not since she was little when she always tossed her cook-ies without warning. This time I wouldn't have blamed her if she had. We both stood hyperventilating, hoping the killer wasn't still somewhere nearby.

I scanned the monotone winter landscape for any sign of movement. At the edge of my eye I thought I glimpsed something padding silently among the pines. When I looked, it was gone.

Chapter Thirteen

The hunter's weapon lay several feet away. He'd been trying to shoot at something when the gun was knocked from his hand. As with the other victims, the jugular had been severed, a horrified expression frozen in the deceased's facial features, as though he had seen Satan himself. Minutes passed like hours before Skip arrived with the crime unit. Racing the storm, the forensics team went immediately to work.

"What took you so long?" I said. "I called you over half an hour ago."

"Couldn't find the camera."

He walked around to get a better look at the victim. With a latex-gloved hand he extracted a pigskin wallet from the vest pocket of the hunter's torn jacket.

"Do you know who this is?" he said, sliding the driver's license free of the wallet.

"No, who?"

"Daryl Mason."

"Who's he?"

"Some wealthy Nevada land baron. He owns a string of casinos and thousands of acres of Tahoe property."

"Oh, yeah. I've heard of him. In cahoots with Tallis, isn't...er...wasn't he?"

"Uh, huh." Skip deposited the wallet in a Ziplok bag with the hunter's other personal effects.

"I heard Tallis is also planning to build a shopping mall smack in the middle of the Washoe's traditional summer home on the West Shore."

Skip sighed. "Just what we need. Another tribal uprising."

He snapped several photos of the body from various

angles.

"This scene looks an awful lot like the others, Skip."

"I'd have to agree with you there. And whoever or whatever did this much damage had to be pretty large."

"And powerful!" I added.

"The coroner's reports are in on the first two stiffs, by the way."

"And?"

"The victims were already dead before they were mutilated."

"How did they determine that?"

"Their hearts literally exploded. They were run to the ground like frightened rabbits."

"I guess that could explain the extreme facial rigor."

"Better keep this information under your beanie, though, Beanie. If you print that tidbit in the Times, we could have a full-scale panic on our hands."

"I'll try."

"The headline I saw this morning isn't going to help matters."

"What headline?"

"Here, see for yourself." Skip handed me the creased front page of the Times from his jacket pocket.

When I unfolded the newspaper, the leader on my feature hit me like a brick between the eyes, **TAHOE TER-ROR CLAIMS ANOTHER IN GRISLY SLAYINGS. NO SUSPECTS, YET.**

"I didn't write that headline."

"The phones have been ringing off the hook at the station this morning with reports of everything from missing cats to alien abductions," said Skip. "We've got our hands full as it is with people dropping like flies."

"You can thank Carla Meeks and her brief stint at the National Enquirer for this."

"We can't let all the details of this case become public knowledge or folks might panic."

"Is there something you're not telling me?"

"I'm not sure whether I should tell a nosy reporter."

I grinned. "I promise I'll keep it under wraps, Skip."

"We performed salivary amylase tests on tissue samples from the victims."

"And?"

"They tested positive."

"Positive for what?"

"Let me finish, will ya? We found animal saliva in the samples."

"What kind of animal?"

"Dog, I think." Skip scratched his chin.

"You *think*?"

"Well, there were some inconsistencies in the tests. The results were inconclusive."

"If it is an animal, as you say, how did it open the front door at Caruso's place?"

"Beats me. Maybe Caruso left it open."

"Doesn't seem likely, since the place had more alarm systems than Fort Knox. Was the door open when the police arrived?"

"I don't think so, but evidence doesn't lie. And there's another odd thing."

"What's that, Skip?"

"Missing shoes."

"I don't follow you."

"Remember when Robson was discovered, a shoe was found near the body?"

"Yeah, so? You found a beat up shoe. It wasn't Robson's, right?"

"On the contrary..."

"But he was wearing both his shoes."

"While conducting a search of his house, we discovered a shoe missing from a shoe box in the closet. We didn't think much of it until we discovered the same thing at Caruso's place. A Farragamo loafer. I'll wager our hunter here is missing one, too."

A bell went off in my brain like one of Tom's fire alarms. Skip was definitely onto something here. I had a theory of my own simmering on the back burner, but I wasn't ready to share it. Not yet. What I didn't know then was this was all coming to a rolling boil a lot sooner than I thought.

The flash from the camera lit the tree trunks in the vicinity. As if in answer, a lightning flash illuminated the black clouds, and thunder grumbled in the distance. Moments later, lacy white flakes began to dust our jackets.

"By the way, where's Nona?" Skip asked as he aimed the camera once more at the victim's remains before the coroner zipped up the body bag.

"She decided to wait in the car. She's pretty upset."

"Can't say I blame her."

"You know how protective I've always been where Nona's concerned."

"Don't beat yourself up about it, Beanie. You're a good mom, but you can't protect your kids forever."

"I know. It doesn't keep you from wanting to, though."

"I wish we had even one reliable lead on these killings," he said.

"Me, too."

"Dog spit's not much to go on, and I'm guessing the killer isn't named Imelda."

"Don't forget, Skip, the victims all had something else in common."

"What?"

"They were all connected to Tallis one way or another."

"Whoever or whatever it is, I hope we close in soon. I'm getting tired of chasing my tail, and Stoddard's getting more impatient by the minute."

"I have an upset young lady out in the car who's probably getting pretty impatient to leave."

"I think we'd all better high-tail it before this storm gets any worse." Skip glanced skyward and pulled up his collar against the howling wind. Was it only the wind? "Anyway, our ex-land baron here has a date with the medical examiner."

"Call me later."

"Will do."

As we drove away from the scene back out to Highway 89, I wasn't sure whether or not Nona was in shock. Her eyes were fixed straight ahead, and she spoke not a word. When I saw a tear spill down her cheek, I knew she would be all right.

"That was so totally gross!" she said.

"I'm sorry, Nona. I wanted so much for our day together to be perfect. I never dreamed anything like this would happen."

"Just how involved are you in this investigation, Mom?"

"I told you. I'm covering it for the Times."

"Tell the truth. I think you're up to your earflaps in this."

My silence was all the answer she needed. I had to admit she was right. It had become more than stringing articles for the Times and snooping around for Skip. Only now Nona was involved, too. Did I dare tell her what I really thought about all this? What I really believed might be at the center of it? If I did, she'd think her mother was nuttier than a Nestle's Crunch Bar, and maybe she'd be right.

"Well," I changed horses midstream, "how would my glamour girl like to pick out a new dress for the Fireman's Ball? My treat."

"Really? When?"

"We'll see, okay?"

"Okay."

I felt relieved to see a smile tilt the corners of her mouth and renewed sparkle in her ginger snap eyes. My diversionary tactic worked. By the time we pulled into the driveway, all thoughts of murder scenes and mother-daughter quarrels were far behind us, at least for a little while.

Cruiser saw us drive up and met us at the door. I'd emptied him out before I left, but apparently he'd spent too much time at the water bowl while we were gone. The moment I opened the front door, he barreled past us, waded chest deep to Ye Olde Piddling Pine, and saluted it with a hind leg. I felt terrible for making him wait so long.

"That does it," I said. "We're getting you a doggy door." Cruiser looked up at me as if to say, *Now, there's a capital idea! What took you so long to think of it?*

That evening the fire felt heavenly after our harrowing ski trip. We'd decided to postpone our shop-a-thon because after the day's events, we were both about to drop. Nona and I lounged on the couch reading, with Cruiser tucked comfortably between us. We propped our feet on opposite ends of the ottoman, our toes roasting like plump marshmallows before the flames in the rustic stone fireplace. The storm gathered force, and the wind shrieked around the cabin's edifice, tugging at the stalwart pines as though to uproot them. Cruiser seemed restless, and his long ears pricked up as though he heard something...something only he could hear.

"Settle down, boy. It's only the wind." But he didn't settle down. "Do you need to go potty?" I asked, but he didn't seem interested in moving from the couch. I set my latest article draft aside and stood up to stretch my stiff muscles. "I'm getting drowsy. Would you like some coffee, Nona?"

"Know what sounds even better?"

"What?"

"Hot chocolate. With mounds of real whipped cream like you used to make for Pop and me when I was little."

"You said the magic word."

"What?"

"Chocolate. I'll go fix some. I don't have any whipping cream, but I have some Cool Whip in the fridge."

"That'll do fine. Better get another log or two for the fire while you're at it. It's dying down."

"Will do."

"Need any help, Mom?"

"Nah, I can handle it. You just stay cozy here and keep Cruiser company." It was good to finally have Nona to myself for awhile, without Medwyn horning in on our time together.

I stepped into the kitchen. Flicking on the light, I shoved the iron doorstop aside and nudged the swinging door shut behind me so Cruiser wouldn't follow me to beg for biscuits. I found a box of instant hot chocolate mix in the cupboard. Only two packets were left. I'd have to pick up some more when I went to buy Cruiser's new dog door. Fortunately, I always keep a good supply of milk on hand for a chocolate chip cookie chaser or hot chocolate. I've never cared for cocoa made with water. It tastes too wimpy.

The window over my kitchen sink faces the forest. Tom had the house built that way for me. I get my best ideas when I'm washing dishes, so I wanted a view of the woods while I'm standing at the sink. I wasn't prepared for the view I got this night. I had just knelt down to get a saucepan from the cupboard beneath the stove. When I stood up and

faced the window, what I saw through the glass turned my
blood to ice. I let out a scream that brought Nona running on
the double. Cruiser trotted behind her into the kitchen to see
what was the matter. He yelped in surprise when the door
bopped him in the rump as it swung closed behind him.

Chapter Fourteen

"Mom! Are you okay?"

"Y...yes."

"You scared me half to death. I thought you were hurt."

I reached up and yanked down the window shade.

"What is it?" Nona asked.

"I saw something at the window just now."

"What?"

"I'm not sure."

"You're scaring me, Mom. What *was* it?"

"I told you, I don't know. I only got a glimpse, then it was gone." Cruiser sensed the fear in my voice and pawed my leg. I felt frightened for all of us. I couldn't explain what I'd seen at my window, except it was huge and terrifying. And those glowering eyes! I believed what lurked outside our very door was the Tahoe Terror, whatever *it* was.

I heard the crack of a limb and a thud against the cabin's exterior. Then, the lights went out, and we were enveloped in darkness. I tried to walk to the wall telephone, but I couldn't seem to make my limbs work, like in a bad dream. When Cruiser pointed his muzzle toward the ceiling to bay in answer to a preternatural wailing somewhere outside, I knew it was time to call out the Mounties.

My index finger trembled as I fumbled to punch 911 on the unlit buttons of the receiver. It took me a second to realize the phone was dead.

"Nona, where's your cellular?"

"In my backpack."

"Where's the backpack?"

"In the living room, I think."

Stumbling in the dark kitchen toward the door, I

couldn't see Cruiser lying right in my path. Who needs an obstacle course when you have a basset in the house? When I stepped on his tail, he yelped in pain and jumped to his feet. My right foot hooked on his underside. Then I yelped in pain when I fell forward and landed hard on the linoleum floor, nearly braining myself on the doorstop. My lungs deflated like a stomped-on squeaky toy.

"Mom! What happened? Are you all right?"

I couldn't answer. I lay wheezing like an asthmatic on a hayride. In the darkness, Nona groped for me but found only empty air. Like a slow-motion replay of a football touchdown, I scrambled to my feet and feinted to the right of the furry, slobbering bruiser in my path. I made a dash through the kitchen door to score a field goal in the living room, only to discover the backpack and the cellular phone were still out in the car.

"Sorry, Mom," Nona said, standing in the living room with me. "I thought I brought it in with me."

"It's okay, honey," I said, rubbing my knee. "The lights should be back on in a minute." Speed bump Cruiser was still in the kitchen howling like a...well, like a basset hound.

Every kid knows monsters are afraid of the light. Every horror movie ever made affirmed that in our impressionable young minds. What those bad B movies never taught us is what to do in similar real-life situations.

Usually, the bimbo wearing the wispy negligee either walked right into the waiting arms of the beast or let it sneak up on her from behind through an open window or door. Well, these two bimboes and a basset were staying put. The doors and windows were locked tighter than a Scotsman's purse. Whatever peered at me through the window moments before was still somewhere outside, and I prayed it would stay there.

Like in the movies, we'd huddle together and wait for daylight to chase away the long-leggetty beasties and things that go bump in the night. I was glad I hadn't installed Cruiser's dog door yet.

Nona and I hadn't slept together in the same bed since she was a little girl. With the storm shrieking outside our door, along with who knew what else, we were both glad to have company. So was Cruiser, the big chicken. When we awoke the next morning, I was hanging off the edge of the bed, and Nona dangled off the other side. Right in the middle, belly up and snoring contentedly, lay our fearless protector.

"Come on, you lazy, worthless hound," I said. "Time to get up and go water the pine." Cruiser yawned and stretched before finally relinquishing his cherished spot on the bed. Before he could change his mind, Nona rolled over to reclaim the bed and catch a few more winks.

I opened the door an inch or two, fearing what I might find on my doorstep. All I saw outside was another sunless day. It had stopped snowing. Everything seemed so normal I almost forgot last night's events ever happened. Surely, my imagination had been running amok, as it often does, or I'd been reading too many Stephen King novels. Besides, there were no such things as monsters, at least not in broad daylight.

As I escorted Cruiser to the trail of the lonesome pine, I noticed the woods seemed strangely silent. Even on dreary winter mornings, I usually hear jays squawking or chipmunks chattering. Had something scared them away? Worse yet, did something still lurk close by? The chill coursing up my spine wasn't from my soaking wet feet.

"Hurry up, Cruiser!" I commanded.

Finally, he answered my call, looking like a fat caterpillar as he humpity-humped through the snowdrifts. As I waited for him to navigate the last few feet to the front door, I noticed the imprints in the snow, partially obliterated by last night's snowfall. They led right to my kitchen window.

I was relieved to hear a dial tone when I picked up the phone and even more relieved to hear Skip's friendly voice on the other end when I got through to the Sheriff's office.

"Hey, Beanie. What's up?"

"We had a prowler here last night."

"Why on earth didn't you call me then?"

"Couldn't. The storm knocked out the phone."

"But I thought Nona had a cellular."

"She left it in the car. We were stranded."

"Did you see anything?"

"You bet your brass badge, I did. Something scared the wits out of us last night, and this morning I found prints in the snow. They're massive!"

"I'll come out and have a look around."

"We'll be waiting for you. I'm just about to brew some coffee."

"Say, how about frying me up a couple of eggs, too. Sunny side up."

"Who do you think I am? That dish from Debbie's Diner, Rita Ramirez?"

Skip guffawed, then hung up the phone.

Standing at the sink, I pulled up the shade a few inches and peered out. "Looks like the sun is trying to break through those clouds for our walk, Cruiser." When I remembered those eyes peering back at me, I yanked the shade right back down.

Chapter Fifteen

Skip seemed to take forever outside. I doubted if he would find much, but I hadn't imagined the creature at my window or those cold, yellow eyes staring at me like Skip's eggs on the plate, which were cold, too. I put them in the oven to warm. Nona finally emerged from the bedroom, poured herself some coffee and sat down at the table to eat her oatmeal.

"I seem to recall someone saying she was going to take me shopping," Nona said, pouring cream into her coffee. Apparently, last night's events hadn't made as much of an impression on her as they had on me.

"Uh, huh," I answered, stirring my oatmeal.

"What's wrong, Mom?"

"Oh, nothing."

"Still thinking about last night?"

"Yes."

"What do you think it was, anyway?"

"I don't know. Maybe Skip can tell us, if he ever finishes out there."

"I thought I heard Skip's voice. What's he doing here?"

"He just dropped by to...uh...check things out."

"We were both tired and stressed by what happened at Kiva, Mom. I think your imagination was just playing tricks on you."

"I don't think so."

"Well, it was probably just a bear. You said you've seen them mooching around here before in the winter."

"Maybe you're right. Let's forget about it for now, okay? Eat your oatmeal. It's getting cold." I was doing it again. Treating her like a child, spoon-feeding her the truth like I used to spoon-feed her oatmeal. I dusted some granola on my cereal. We both ate in silence. Silence begging to be broken.

"Something else is bothering you," Nona said. "I can always tell, so 'fess up."

I was busted. Might as well come clean, I thought. At least halfway. "Well, I wasn't going to worry you, but I saw some strange prints in the snow this morning when I took Cruiser for his constitutional. We didn't just imagine what happened last night, Nona. There really *was* something out there."

"Yeah. So Yogi forgot to take his winter nap. He was probably just hungry and came down to raid the garbage can." I knew Nona didn't believe that 100%. She was just trying to convince herself we hadn't really been in mortal danger.

"I don't think it was a bear," I said.

"A coyote, then."

"Too small."

"Well, what else could it have been? Those are the only big animals I've ever seen around here, besides Cruiser."

Cruiser looked up momentarily from his rapidly emptying bowl of diet kibble, then resumed eating.

"Do you remember the stories Grandpop used to tell you when you were little?"

"You mean the ones about our Washoe ancestors?"

"Mm, hm."

"How could I forget? Who needs Big Bird when you've got the terrible Ang. And Hanglwuiwui, the man-eating giant. Grandpop used to scare the bejezus out of me when he told those tales, especially when we went camping." Gooseflesh freckled Nona's arms.

"I remember," I laughed. "You used to tuck so far down in your mummy bag all we could see were a pair of saucer eyes peeking out the top."

"I was afraid the Ang bird might swoop down and carry me off."

"Oh, Nona." I laughed.

"But you don't really believe those tall tales, do you, Mom? They're just what you said, legends."

I was prepared for Nona's skepticism. After all, what

would you expect from a platinum card-carrying member of Generation X? At least she hadn't told me I was completely nutso.

"Probably safe to assume it's not the Ang or Hanglwuiwui, but let's just say I'm keeping an open mind." I felt my own flesh tingle as I thought again of the glowering eyes I saw outside my window, and the footprints in the snow I discovered outside my very door. Those weren't just goose bumps swimming up my arms but a flock of honking ganders.

Just then I heard Skip kicking the snow off his boots at the back door.

"Man, that snow's getting deep out there," Skip said.

"It's getting deep in here, too," Nona cracked.

"Leave your boots outside, will ya? I don't want snow melting all over my wood floors."

Skip slipped off his cop clodhoppers and padded into the kitchen in his woolly socks.

"Hi, Nona. How's it goin'?" Skip said, pouring himself some coffee.

"Fine, Skip." Nona smoothed her hair. She's always conscious of her appearance when a man is present, even if it's only Skip.

"Can't complain...much."

"Your breakfast was ready ages ago," I said. "It's warming in the oven. Better use the mitt or you'll burn yourself."

"Sorry I took so long. I just wanted to have a good look around."

"Find anything interesting?" Nona said, winking. "Like a Hanglwuiwui?"

"A *what*?!" Skip sputtered through a mouthful of coffee.

"Thanks a bunch, big mouth," I chided Nona.

"Go on, Mom. Tell him what you just told me. Go on."

"Oh, all right. Stop goading me like your father used to."

Skip wiped coffee drips off his shirt with a napkin. "Tell me what?"

"Well, I was just reminding Nona about the legends

her great grandfather used to tell her."

"Yeah, so?" Skip scooped an egg whole into his mouth and swallowed it. And I thought Tom was a speed eater.

"Mom thinks something supernatural was lurking outside her kitchen window last night. Wee-ooo!"

"Yeah, and I'm from Planet Hollyweird. Sheesh. You girls have been watching too many cheesy horror flicks."

"I didn't say that exactly, but I saw something pretty strange."

"I think it was more likely a rogue bear. I wouldn't worry about it if I were you."

I could see I was fighting a losing battle trying to convince Skip and Nona. Skip emptied his coffee cup and wiped his mouth on the back of his hand. "Thanks for the breakfast."

"Sure, anytime."

Skip stretched and yawned. "Well, I'd better hightail it back to the office. Stoddard will be on the warpath if I'm not back soon. In the meantime, you girls keep your doors locked at all times, just in case."

"Tighter than a scout's knot," I said.

"Yeah, you never know if there might be a Louie, Louie hangin' around."

"That's a Hanglwui..."

The door clicked shut behind him. I could still hear Skip laughing as he walked to his car.

After Skip left, I got up and walked to the cupboard.

"What are you looking for, Mom?"

"Aspirin? You got any? I'm getting one of those headaches."

"Sure." Nona fished in her purse and handed me a tin of Motrin. "Here."

I gulped two capsules with a java chaser. Maybe all the mayhem of this strange case was starting to get to me more than I thought. Or perhaps this was just perimenopause at its best. If so, somebody please pass the wild yam cream.

Chapter Sixteen

The sun broke through a veil of gray clouds and scattered the shadows. The warmth beating through the windshield of the Jeep felt good. Nona's and my shopping spree at Velvet and Lace had helped my headache subside, so I decided to continue driving to The Haute Hydrant to buy Cruiser's dog door.

We drove past the only skyscrapers in South Tahoe, the casinos clustered at Stateline, their neon signs pulsing even in the daytime. I don't gamble much any more. I used to shake hands with a few one-armed bandits years ago when I came to visit my parents, but after I moved up here so close to temptation, making rich men richer and me poorer soon lost its luster. I confess I've ventured a few quarters trying to win the red Mercedes Benz convertible at The Colosseum, Tahoe's newest casino. Dream on, Beanie.

I pulled into the parking lot of Round Hill's minimall housing The Haute Hydrant and parked in front of the shop. *DUTCH BUNNIES 4 SALE $10.99*, read the sign in bold lettering over the display window, where a multicolored ball of fuzzy bunnies snuggled ear-to-ear in a sunny corner. Teddy bear hamsters cavorted in cedar chip moguls in the adjoining cage.

"You coming in with me, Nona?"

"No, I'll just wait here and soak up some sun."

"Okay, I shouldn't be too long."

The Hydrant seemed quiet for a Saturday, until I stepped inside. The moment I opened the door, a discordant symphony of chirping parakeets and squawking parrots all but drowned out the proprietor's only alarm system, a yappy Yorkshire terrier named Fabian.

"Hi, Beanie. No Cruiser?" said Sally Applebaum.

"I didn't bring him along today. Besides, once he got a whiff of all these incredible edibles, I'd never get him out of here."

"Has he eaten all his diet dog food already?"

"No, he's going to take awhile to polish that off. Not quite as enthusiastic about it as his old chow."

"Well, if you want to go back to the Hi-Pro formula, you'll have to put in an order for it. I'm fresh out."

"Oh?"

"We seem to have had a run on dog food here lately. It's literally flying off the shelves."

"Could be all the skiers who bring their Newfies and Great Pyrenees to Tahoe with them for the holidays."

"Oh, I never thought of that. Those are big dogs, all right."

"Speaking of big dogs, do you have any doors to fit a short-legged moose?"

Sally laughed. "Well, not a moose, exactly, but I have a pretty large one."

"Great!"

"Follow me. I'll show you what I have."

I followed Sally down the main aisle, stopping briefly to cuddle some Guinea pigs.

"Here you are." Sally held up a large, flat box with one of those funny-looking dogs on it. You guessed it, a basset hound.

"Cruiser should be able to fit through this just fine," I said. *But hopefully no monsters,* I thought. I flipped the box over and examined the specifications on the back. "Does it have a lock?"

"Yes, there's a sturdy security panel you can fasten on, so you don't have to worry about intruders finding their way through it when you're not at home."

Or when you are.

"It even has magnets to hold the vinyl flap in place and keep drafts out. Installation is easy, too. Just cut a hole in your door, attach the dog door with the screws, and you're all set."

"How much is it?"

"This size is $119.99."

"Whew. Not cheap, is it?"

"No, but it's quality made."

"Well, I guess it's worth it if Cruiser can find his own way outside. I'm tired of being doorman for a dog."

"Going to the Fireman's Ball tonight?" Sally asked as she waited for me to write my check.

"Yes. Nona and I have tickets," I said, nodding toward the car outside. "We've been dress shopping."

"Oh, Nona's visiting for the holidays? How nice." Sally waved at Nona through the window with one hand as she tapped the keys on the register with the other.

"How about you, Sally?"

"Beg pardon?" Sally looked up momentarily.

"Are you going to the ball?"

"Me? Oh, no," she said.

"Well, there's always next year."

Her cheery demeanor suddenly faded. "I think I'd better keep a close eye on things here, anyway."

"Why? Anything wrong?"

"Had a prowler a couple of nights ago."

"You did?"

"I was in the stock room taking inventory, when I heard Fabian barking his little head off. The rest of the animals were going crazy, too."

"Did you see anything?"

"When I came up front to investigate all the commotion, I saw a silhouette through the front door shade."

"Could you see who it was?"

"No, not clearly. I was afraid to get too close. I didn't want the intruder to know I was here alone."

"Didn't you call 911?"

"Luckily, whoever it was went away, so I didn't bother to report it."

I shivered, remembering what I'd seen at my own window. "Well, be careful here alone tonight, Sal."

"I will."

"If you see anything else strange, call the Sheriff's office."

"Will do." Sally bagged up my purchase and dropped some dog treat samples in the bag. "Here you go, Beanie. I hope Cruiser enjoys his new door," Sally said, handing me my change. "You two have a great time at the dance."

"We will, thanks."

"See you later."

"You bet, Sal. Take care."

Sally smiled and waved good-bye. I could hear Fabian still yipping his yappy little alarm as we drove away.

"Gosh, it's nearly two o'clock already," Nona said. "Where did the day go?"

"Time flies when you're spending money," I said.

"By the way, thanks for the dress, Mom. It's so pretty."

"I'm sure you'll be the belle of the ball in it, honey."

"What time does the dance start?"

"Not 'til seven. We still have plenty of time to get ready. In fact, I think I may have enough time to install Cruiser's new door, if I hurry."

"Need any help?"

"Nah. I've gotten pretty handy around the house. Without your dad around, I had to. Skip lends me a hand sometimes, if I really need it."

"He's a good friend to you, isn't he?"

"Sure is."

Nona patted my hand. "I'm glad, Mom. I don't like to think of you getting lonely up here all by yourself."

"I've always been all right on my own, but sometimes it gets pretty quiet at the cabin, even with my basset buddy around. I'm so glad you could come up for Thanksgiving. I still miss your father a lot, especially during the holidays."

"I know. I miss him, too."

We both looked straight ahead so we wouldn't see the tears welling in each other's eyes.

"See, boy? A brand new doggy door just for you!"

Cruiser cocked his head, clearly puzzled by the new contraption I had installed in the back door.

"Lookie, here!" I nudged the vinyl flap a few times to give him the idea he could push it with his nose, if he were so inclined.

He looked at me like I'd finally flipped my ever-lovin' beanie.

I nudged the door open wider, but it still wasn't sinking in on Cruiser exactly what I expected him to do. I wondered why on earth the company who made this door would have put a basset hound on the front of their box to advertise it. What would ever make them think a basset could learn to use one?

"I know what will work." I went to Cruiser's yum-yum nook and retrieved the one thing that would make him romance a flaming porcupine, let alone perform a simple feat like walking through a dog door. I opened the back door, then reached through the vinyl flap, waving the secret weapon. "Oh, Cru-u-uiser. Look. Bacon Beggin' Strip." Quick as lightning, Cruiser snapped the treat from my fingers, and I drew back a slobbery hand. I tried again, only this time I held the flap up and waved the strip on the outside. "Come on, Cruiser. Come on, boy."

Ah! Success, at last. Cruiser nudged the flap once or twice. Finally, out came one paw, then another, and the hind end followed suit. "Atta boy. Good dog," I gave him his reward. Except I was the one who deserved a reward for a performance well done.

"Well, how do I look?" Nona said, modeling her new dress for me as I hot-curled my salt and pepper hair. I saw myself thirty years earlier, if I squinted my eyes hard enough. The turquoise chiffon brushing against her burnished skin was an azure sky against the tawny earth of a western plain, her chestnut hair a sunset on Mount Tallac.

"You're a vision, honey." I sighed, feeling proud of Tom's and my legacy, our beautiful daughter, Wenona. I so wished he were here to share my pride. The blending of our cultures had produced a rare gem in her.

"What's that funny smell?" Nona asked.

"An odd scent filled the room; something was burning. I glanced around the bedroom, but there wasn't a flaming porcupine in sight. In the mirror I spotted smoke signals rising from my head.

"My hair!" I screeched, unwrapping my smoldering hair from the curling iron. The end of the fried curl came off in my hand. "Now look what I've done."

"Don't worry. I'll fix it." Nona took a brush and expertly blended the damaged lock.

"Thanks, honey. No one will be able to tell I nearly cooked myself."

"You look pretty, Mother. I didn't know you had such a fancy dress."

"Oh, I keep it around, just in case." I did a respectable model's pirouette in my red satin evening gown.

"I'm accustomed to seeing you in denim and flannel."

The look of pride in Nona's eyes was not lost on me.

"Well, maybe we'll have to double date more often; then I'll have an excuse to dress up once in a while." I gave her a playful peck on the cheek.

"Now if I can just find my other red shoe."

"What should I do with my hair, Mom?"

"Just wear it down." I got down on all fours to look under the bed. Cruiser thought it was playtime. He ambled up and gave me a slurp right on the end of my nose. "Cruiser, do ya mind?" I said, nudging him aside. "I already washed my face."

"But I wanted to do something different with it for this evening."

"What on Earth did I do with that shoe?"

"Maybe Cruiser took it," Nona said.

"Cruiser might be a lot of things, but shoe-chewer isn't one of them."

"Did you look in the closet?"

"Of course I did."

"Could it be in another shoe box?"

I might be getting a bit dotty in my dotage, I thought, but I wasn't blind. I could still match my shoes.

"No, I've looked. It's just not here. Guess I'll just have to wear the black ones, instead."

"Forget the shoes, and come help me style my hair," Nona said.

I slipped into my black patent pumps, disappointed that my perfect ensemble would be incomplete. "Hand me the brush. Let's experiment a little."

"Okay. Only, no curling irons, please. I don't want to go to the dance bald."

Chapter Seventeen

Only the flashing lights of the casinos could outshine the thousands of stars above, diamonds you could almost pluck from the velvety night sky. The Colosseum's lot was nearly full, but we managed to find a parking space. As Nona and I walked across the lot, I could see Skip waiting for us at the entrance. He flashed his Ray Bolger grin, but he didn't look anything like a scarecrow tonight in his blue suit that complemented his blue eyes and ruddy cheeks. His usually tousled sandy hair was parted arrow straight and Brylcreemed. A brisk scent of Old Spice aftershave filled the air. Even his shoes looked like they'd had some extra spit and polish for the occasion. I was impressed and rather flattered by his efforts.

"You two look like a million bucks!" Skip said.

"You don't look so shabby yourself," I said. "New threads?"

"Uh, huh."

"Lookin' mighty sharp, Skip." I smiled as he offered me his arm like a gentleman and escorted me inside the casino. I felt caught a little off-guard by his sudden charm. Perhaps it had been too long since I'd gone out on a date. Is that what this was?

Nona hurried across the casino. Skip and I followed. The music of The Twilite Trio drifted out the open door of the Grand Showroom as we queued up in the line that snaked down the dimly lit carpeted hallway.

"I don't see you dressed to the nines very often, Beanie. You should dress up more often."

"And leave my deerstalker at home?" I nudged him playfully in the ribs, thinking of my singed hair, thankful I hadn't needed to wear a hat.

"Mom, what's this stuff on your dress?" Nona said.

"What?" I glanced down at the powdery substance on the satin. "Have I ruined my one good dress?" When I touched it, the powder felt kind of slippery between my fingers like serpentine in my college geology class.

"Hey, Beanie, look. You're glowing in the dark."

"You *are*, Mom!"

"What do you suppose it is?" Nona brushed the strange powder off my skirt as best she could, but some residue remained. "Well, I'll be a glow-in-the-dark Beanie Baby," I laughed.

My joking seemed to alter Skip's Prince Charming mood. I felt disappointed when the silly party banter shifted suddenly to police business. He pulled me aside in the line.

"I have something to talk to you about later."

"Sure."

"By the way, where's you know who?"

"You mean Medwyn?"

"Yeah."

"Nona said he's meeting her here. Oh, I almost forgot. Here's your ticket, Skip."

"Thanks. What do I owe you?"

"Twenty-five."

"Twenty-five dollars! I didn't know the tickets cost so much."

"Neither did I, but since it's for a good cause I bought four of them, anyway." My attempt at sarcasm was completely lost on him.

"Pay you back later for my ticket, okay?"

"Yeah, sure thing." So much for Prince Charming.

By the time we were finally ushered to our seats, the dance floor already overflowed with folks paired up like passengers on Noah's forty-day love cruise. Sequins on the ladies' gowns glinted in the sparkling lights reflected from the mirrored ball spinning above their heads. I thought of Tom and me when we took cha-cha lessons at Arthur Murray. Then our first date and my go-go boots came to mind. I laughed to myself. I was glad to see I had dressed appropriately for this occasion, even if my shoes didn't match my dress; I sure didn't need any sequins on it to shine in the dark. I was still puzzled over the odd stain on my dress and my missing red shoe. I'd have to have a chat with Cruiser if he'd developed a taste for shoe leather on his new slimming diet. My good shoes were not about to become his new rawhide chewies.

Patrons were lined up for drinks at the no-host bar, several already looking like they'd had one too many for the road. The slow dance finished, and the band broke into a lounge lizard rendition of "Twist and Shout." John Lennon surely twisted and shouted in his grave as the Trio's chunky lead singer belted out the lyrics of the Beatles' classic 60s song.

"Care to dance?" Skip said. He stood and offered his hand, bowing as though he were Sir Walter Raleigh.

"Why not?" I said, half expecting him to throw his coat on the floor for me to walk across.

We waded through a sea of squirming bodies until we found enough space to move in. I managed to avoid getting poked in the eye or having my foot stomped on by the middle-aged guy next to me doing the Freddy, or the Frug, or whatever he was doing, with such exuberance.

Fortunately, the music ended before I needed the paramedics, and we exited the dance floor in one piece.

"Would you like a drink, Beanie?"

"Yes, please!" I said, fanning my face with a cocktail menu. "I can use one after that Tae Bo workout."

"What'll it be?"

"A strawberry margarita."

"Frozen or on the rocks?"

"Frozen. No salt."

"Be right back."

As Skip disappeared into the crowd, I saw Nona marching toward me. She plopped down in the chair across from me and locked her arms across her chest. Her face was flushed.

"Nona, what's wrong?" I asked.

"It's Medwyn. He's not coming."

"He's probably just a little late."

"No! I called him to see why he's not here yet. He's definitely not coming."

"Did he say why?"

"Something about business."

"On a Saturday night?"

"I didn't believe him, either. God, I hate being stood up."

"Have I scared another one away, honey?" Suddenly I felt guilty about the way I had treated Medwyn, and the way Cruiser bit him.

"Forget it, Mom. I guess he's just another Mr. Wrong." A tear rolled down her pretty bronze cheek.

I handed her a tissue from my purse. "Don't be upset, Nona. Perhaps he really did have business to attend to." I couldn't believe I was actually defending the jerk.

"I doubt it. And what makes me maddest is you bought me this nice dress for nothing."

"What do you mean? There are lots of other nice-looking young men here."

"Yeah? I don't see too many of them standing in a stag line, do you?"

I looked around the room, searching desperately for a handsome, unattached man. Nona was right. There wasn't a stag line or a lonely guy in sight.

"Cheer up, honey. I'm sure someone will ask you to dance. Anyway, Skip will be happy to dance with you." Nona didn't look too thrilled at the prospect. Only one thing would have cheered her up. To see Medwyn Abercarn walk in. Somehow, I figured the odds were greater of me winning that red Mercedes Benz out in the casino.

"I think I'll just go on home. Can I take the car, Mom?"

"I wish you'd stay, Nona."

"I have a headache."

"I understand, dear. I'll get a ride home with Skip."

"Thanks."

When I saw more tears trail down Nona's cheeks, I knew it wasn't a headache but a heartache that sent her hurrying through the crowd. My heart ached, too, when I thought of her big evening being ruined. I know how much she'd been looking forward to it. Men! Definitely from Mars.

"Here's your margarita," Skip said. "Where's Nona?"

"She left."

"How come?"

"Her date stood her up." I took a long swig of iced strawberry margarita, making slurpee sounds at the bottom of the glass.

"Gee, that sucks."

I would have laughed at Skip's pun, but I was too concerned about Nona.

"I knew Medwyn was bad news for Nona the first time I laid eyes on him."

"I don't think he's just bad news for Nona."

My ears perked up, and I stopped sipping. "What do you mean?"

"I mean his connections with Tallis."

"Just what are his connections with Tallis? I've never been very clear about that."

"Apparently, Tallis isn't either."

"Why?"

"I've been trying to contact this guy for days, and every time I call over there, I get forwarded to his voice mail."

"So...? I never get a live human being on the phone any more."

"Well, there aren't too many live human beings left at Tallis."

"This is true."

"There's something else, though, Beanie. Remember the missing shoes?"

"Yeah?"

"Well, I was right about our last victim."

"He's with the one-shoe crew?"

"Yep. I didn't think too much of it at first, but it's the same thing with the other victims."

It wasn't the icy margarita freezing the words in my throat.

"I've got a news flash, Skip. One of *my* shoes is missing, too. The red shoes I planned to wear with this dress tonight. They aren't expensive designer shoes like Caruso's, but..."

"I think it's high time I had a little chat with this Medwyn character, Beanie."

"I think it's time we both had a chat with him."

"By the way, here's the twenty-five dollars I owe

you for the ticket." Skip let the moths fly out of his wallet. "Sheesh, these tickets get more expensive every year."

"Remember, it's for sweet charity."

"I'll try to remember that when I'm on unemployment."

"What do you mean?"

"Stoddard blew his stack at me yesterday. He said if I don't have a suspect collared soon, I'm out."

"Off the case?"

"Off the force."

"No way!"

"Yes way!"

"Stoddard's such a jerk."

"You can say that again."

"Stoddard's such a jerk." My attempt at humor was lame, but I wanted to nudge Skip back into his party mood.

"Say, Beanie, are you attending the meeting Monday night?"

"What meeting?"

"It seems the Tribal Council and Tallis are finally going to have it out over the Cave Rock issue."

"Oh, yeah. I did hear something about a meeting."

"Should be entertaining."

"You're going, too?"

"Have to. Stoddard wants us to be there to referee if things get out of hand, like the other day at his speech."

"Not a bad idea. If you ask me, I think Cave Rock is just the tip of the iceberg."

"Well, if it isn't Officer Cassidy," a sultry voice crooned.

We both turned at the same time to find ourselves abreast, so to speak, with Rita Ramirez. I saw sweat bead instantly on Skip's temples when he got an eyeful of Rita's daring décolletage. She was as tipsy as a cork.

"R...R...Rita," Skip stammered. I wondered he got that much out with his mouth hanging open.

"Skippy, what a nice surprise!"

"Uh..., likewise."

"Hi," Rita said, casting me a side-glance.

I nodded.

"Did you come alone?" Skip asked just a little too eagerly. Sir Walter would never have done that to Queen Liz.

"Nope. I'm here with your boss."

"Stoddard's here?"

"Uh, huh," Rita said, pointing to a nearby table where Stoddard sat glaring at us between gulps of Scotch.

"Oh, great. Just what I need," Skip muttered.

"He asked me out, and since you didn't, well..."

"But I thought you said you were working tonight."

I shot Skip a look that could have melted his badge, if he'd been wearing it. So, I wasn't his first choice for a date, after all.

"No. Monday night. After I'm off, why don't you and I...?" She stopped mid-sentence when she noticed the look on my face. Fortunately for Skip, he noticed the look on my face, too, and for once, buttoned his lip. Rita wasn't throwing in the dish towel so easily. She batted her eyes, ran her fingers through her scarlet hair, and simpered, "I just came over to see if you'd care to have a dance, Skippy."

Skip didn't have to mull it over. Before you could say flapjack floozy, he was out on the dance floor, doing his best disco imitation of John Travolta, because he certainly had Saturday Night Fever.

I saw Stoddard ambling toward Skip and Rita to re-claim his date. I didn't like the look on his face. In fact, I didn't like his face at all.

"Well, well. If it isn't ol' Hopalong Cashidy." Stoddard looked more looped than a roller coaster.

Skip shot an angry glance in the direction of the taunt. Only one person ever called him that.

"Can't you see we're in the middle of a dance here?" Skip said.

"Step aside, Hopalong. I'm cuttin' in." Stoddard yanked Rita away, knocking the wind from her as he clapped her to him.

Skip just stood there alone on the dance floor for a moment. I could see his color rising along with his anger and embarrassment as Stoddard and Rita did a kind of stumbling war dance around him.

"Where's your six-shooter, Hoppy?" Rita cackled.

I thought I saw steam spout from Skip's ears. I had never felt so sorry for him. I instinctively wanted to go out on the floor and intervene, but I decided I'd better let him fight his own battle with his boss.

"Hopalong! Oh, Ho-o-p-along!" Stoddard persisted.

It took everything Skip had not to flatten Stoddard right then and there. Rita sashayed over to Skip and hooked her tentacles around his neck. When Stoddard jerked Rita away from Skip again, he lost his balance and fell over, hitting his eye on the edge of one of the tables. He lay motionless on the dance floor. Several dancers stopped to rubberneck.

"Hey, isn't he the guy who's running for mayor?" I overheard a bystander say.

"Yeah. It's Sheriff Stoddard," answered another.

"Well, he's drunk as a skunk."

When Stoddard didn't move, we began to fear he might be dead. Then he stirred and managed to rise to his hands and knees. Skip helped him to his feet.

"You've had too much to drink. Why don't you go home and sleep it off."

Stoddard nodded, the consequences of his reckless behavior beginning to sink in. Rita ran over to him, but when he shoved her aside, she staggered off crying and disappeared into the crowd. At the same time, security staff ran in the direction of the disturbance. By the time they arrived, the show was over.

And, yes. Men *are* from Mars!

Chapter Eighteen

The Twilight Trio was still belting out oldies but baddies when we left the dance and strolled through the casino. Skip disappeared into the men's room for a few minutes.

"Everything okay?" I asked when he emerged.

"Fine, just fine."

"My hat's off to you for keeping your cool back there. That took guts."

"You'll never know."

"Guess we'd better go now, huh?" I wanted to drop a few quarters in the slot machines but figured Skip would want to leave after the unpleasant incident with his boss. I couldn't have been more wrong.

"Heck, no! I'm not letting those two spoil our evening. As long as we're here, let's give Lady Luck a whirl."

"Are you sure?"

"Never been more sure of anything in my life."

"You're on." I knew there was a Mercedes waiting for me with "Beanie" personalized plates. Fools rush in.

We lined up at the change booth. I bought a roll of quarters. Skip, last of big spenders, bought dollar tokens. He'd been holding out on me. We agreed to meet in an hour. He headed for the blackjack tables, and I beamed in on the fire engine red Mercedes Benz. Not fifteen minutes passed before I saw Skip going back to the change booth to buy more tokens. And he worried about paying twenty-five dollars for a dance ticket? I thought he might to do a Linda Blair head spin when one of the shapely waitresses in a mini toga sashayed past him, balancing her drink tray expertly in one hand. Maybe I would have to insist that girl-watcher Skip wear horse blinders the next time we went out together.

After an hour, and another margarita, courtesy of Skip, I had developed gambler's wrist and my eyes were getting bleary. I dropped my last three quarters in the progressive poker machine. The electronic dealer drew two cards to my long shot royal flush, when suddenly I became aware of, to quote Edgar A. Poe, "the tintinnabulation that so musically wells, from the bells, bells, bells, bells, bells, bells, bells." A silver fountain of quarters spilled into the metal tray. It took several moments of the musical clatter of hard cash for it to sink in on me that I had won the progressive poker round, a grand total of $19,419.99. Not exactly the red Mercedes, but it would do very nicely, thank you.

"Beanie, you won! You won!" Skip appeared at my side, girls in skimpy togas momentarily forgotten. A crowd gathered around me, the big winner of the night. I felt stunned by my sudden stroke of luck. A sea of envious gamblers clamored around me as I received the big payoff.

I stashed my winnings in my purse, and the crowd parted like the Red Sea. A moment later, I was no longer the center of attention, and patrons dispersed. Already my mind reeled. Should I save the money or spend it? Invest in CD's or play the stock market? The trouble is, the minute you have a little money life gets so complicated. Maybe I should just buy a new car. I would have to settle for something a bit less upscale than a Mercedes Benz. Maybe Nona and I could take a vacation together, instead; we could take the Caribbean cruise Tom and I never did, or go visit his folks in Scotland. I could hardly wait to tell Nona about my big win.

"Well, I think I've had all the luck I'm going to have for one night, Skip. Are you ready to go?"

"Yeah, let's call it a night," he said, stifling a yawn. "I have to work tomorrow."

"On Sunday?"

"Stoddard's got us all working overtime on this case."

"That guy's a real slave driver, isn't he?"

"Ben Hur had it easier rowing in the Roman galleys, but until this case solved, looks like we're in for the long haul. Everyone's eager to see an end to this mayhem."

"I'll second that motion. You hang in there, Skip. Let's blow this joint, okay? And you had better be my bodyguard. I don't want to get mugged on the way out."

"Gangway, you dirty rats!" Skip said in his best James Cagney accent as we descended the escalator and approached the front exit. "See any coppers, Babyface?" he said, looking left, then right as he opened the door for me.

"Just one, schweetheart," I answered in a Bogart lisp.

Chapter Nineteen

Morning came all too quickly. I shouldn't have let Skip buy me a second margarita the night before—I knew darned well I had a one-drink limit. The way my head felt, I knew it would never fit in my deerstalker again.

Vaguely aware of a wet tongue licking my hand, I jerked, unsure at first what it was. I wasn't accustomed to awakening without an 80-pound hound on my chest. Then I realized Cruiser had actually managed to let himself out of his new dog door. I hadn't even felt him get off the bed.

"All right, boy. I'm awake." I gave Cruiser a few strokes. "Say, what's this?" Something rubbed off Cruiser's coat onto my hand. "What have you gotten into now, you naughty boy?"

A slick, fine powder glistened on my fingers. It looked just like the stain on my dress the night before. It must have come off Cruiser when I was on all fours looking for my lost shoe. What could it be? Whatever it was, it meant one thing for sure; I'd have to bathe Cruiser. Never my favorite task. Bath time for bassets always made a mess of the bathroom, the wood floors, and me.

As I shuffled past Nona's room to the bathroom to wash my hands, I noticed her door was still closed, so I didn't disturb her. I figured if she felt half as bad as I did, she probably needed the rest. I tiptoed back past her room to the kitchen to brew the strongest coffee this side of Juan Valdez's plantation. My eyes were still glued shut, and my tongue felt like 30-grit sandpaper.

"Never again, Señorita Margarita," I croaked.

I managed to polish off a bowl of corn flakes and a glass of orange juice. I set down Cruiser's bowl of kibble. He sniffed at it, then flopped down on his haunches.

"Not hungry, Cruiser? Whassa matter, too much shoe leather lately?" When he trotted over to the yum-yum nook, I knew he was just holding out for something better than diet kibble.

I handed over the goodies then poured a cup of coffee. By the time I had finished my first cup, my eyes were nearly open. I wanted to go back to bed, but a certain demanding dog wasn't about to let me off so easy. Cruiser already stood in formation for his morning constitutional. Silly me, I had promised to take him to the meadow.

I jerked on my jeans, a turtleneck sweater, and my parka. On the way out the door I donned my deerstalker. To my surprise, it still fit perfectly. Cruiser reared up impatiently on the passenger side of the Cherokee.

"Sorry, boy. This is about as fast as I'm planning to move today. Better get used to it."

I opened the door and hoisted Cruiser into the seat. He assumed cruising stance, and we were off for the meadow, which is really a cow pasture. As I surveyed the horizon through the windshield, the morning sky was cloudless, tourmaline perfection. In the sun's golden glow, the snowy peaks looked like an ice cream sundae topped with butterscotch syrup.

I've never needed one of those dashboard compasses. Cruiser has an uncanny sense of direction. If I go too far past one of our familiar destinations, he whines and nudges my right arm to let me know I'm off course. When the familiar nudge and whine cued me, I made a quick U-turn. A little too quick for Cruiser. He was usually good at leaning into the turns, but not this time. His front end suddenly hit the floorboard. The back half ended up in my lap, with his tail lashing my face. He managed to right himself and shot me a dirty look.

"Sorry, fella. I'll do better next time." I screeched to a stop at the meadow, nearly upending him again, but this time, he dug his claws into the upholstery and hung on. "Okay, we're here."

I helped my shaken companion out of the Jeep and sideslipped down a steep embankment. Cruiser followed at a safe distance, not sure what other shenanigans to expect of his mistress. I slipped under a gap in the barbed wire fence, then held the wire up for Cruiser. We rarely saw any cows in the meadow, but in summer we saw telltale alfalfa pies dotting the broad fields that blended in a watercolor of green and purple with the distant mountains. All we saw on this day were patches of mud where the sun had partially melted the snow.

Cruiser sniffed at the edge of the narrow stream snaking through the meadow. The melting snow had transformed the usually lazy rivulet into respectable rapids. I grew concerned he might fall into the water from the steep bank. Bassets are a lot of things, but good swimmers they're not. I figured we'd already had enough excitement for one day without me fishing an 80-pound dogfish out of the water.

"Cruiser, come!" I called. Of course, true to basset nature, he had no intention of obeying me, at least not until he felt good and ready.

"Cruiser!" A throbbing headache impaired not only my driving ability but my patience. I was in no mood for stubborn bassets.

I stomped toward Cruiser, leash in hand, ready to lasso a certain little wayward doggie. The minute he saw me, he took off in the opposite direction. I ran after him, cursing as I slipped in the snow banks along the creek. He was determined to give me my morning exercise, whether I wanted it or not.

We were rounding another bend in the creek, when through some shrubs along the bank I saw Cruiser freeze in his tracks, then turn tail and run back toward me, Dumbo ears flying. He nearly trampled me as he rounded the foliage. I had never seen him move so fast before, not even for Bacon Beggin' Strips.

I crept past the shrubbery blocking my view to see what had frightened him so. In the glare from the snow, I thought I spotted something ahead. I shaded my eyes from the sun, trying to get a better look. Then I saw it there, drinking at the stream's edge. It stopped drinking and sniffed the air. It hadn't caught my scent. I didn't dare move a muscle. For several moments we were both frozen in our tracks. Cruiser was long gone. As I backed up slowly, the sun blinded me for an instant. When I looked again, the thing was gone. Then I thought I saw someone fleeing through the stand of sugar pines.

Did my eyes deceive me? Had I really seen something there, or was my imagination just playing tricks on me? A chilling cry rose to a crescendo then faded on the winter wind. Impressed in the muddy bank was proof of what I'd swear on my last margarita I'd seen with my own two bloodshot eyes.

***

"Well, I see the dead has finally arisen," I said when Nona shuffled out of the bedroom in her robe and slippers.

"Very funny, Mother. You look a little frazzled. Anything wrong?"

"Cruiser and I had an experience in the meadow this morning."

"What did he do this time?"

"I was chasing after him..."

"So, what else is new?"

"Let me finish, okay?"

Nona entwined her arms in a perturbed pretzel over her breast.

"As I said, I was chasing him along the stream, and then he came running back, scared out of his wits."

"Scared by what? Knowing Cruiser, it was his own shadow."

"Not this time. Try a dog the size of a horse."

"Huh?" Nona dropped her hands to her sides and rolled her eyes. "Really, Mother. How many of those margaritas did you have last night?"

"Not enough to make up a story like that." Or the footprints I saw in the mud. I decided not to tell Nona about those. I didn't want to worry her any further.

"I think you'd better mix up some tomato juice and Tabasco sauce and fix some for that nutty dog of yours, too."

"I know what I saw. Cruiser saw it, too, didn't you, boy?"

Cruiser wagged his tail.

"I'm going back to bed, Mom."

I didn't blame Nona for scoffing at my story. It would seem farfetched to anyone, but I knew what I'd seen.

Too bad my only witness couldn't talk. Nona buttonhooked for the bedroom.

"Wait, Nonie. Why don't you get spruced up, and I'll take you out for your favorite treat."

"Treat?" Nona perked a little at the word.

"What we always did on Sundays when we visited your Gramma and Grampa at Tahoe. Don't you remember?"

"No..."

"Our Sunday sundae. At the soda shop."

"Oh. Thanks, but I don't feel up to it today. I have a headache." *Join the club.*

"I thought you'd want to celebrate."

"Celebrate what?"

"I won a jackpot last night!"

"That's nice, Mom."

Before I could tell her how much I'd won, she headed down the hallway.

"Nona, don't you think you'd feel better if you got out of your bedclothes and showered."

"What's the point?"

"It's daytime is the point."

"I think I'll just go back to bed, if you don't mind."

"Suit yourself."

I would have gone out for a sundae by myself to celebrate my sudden good fortune, but Nona's mood and the strange incident in the pasture had taken the edge off my enthusiasm. I decided I didn't really need the extra calories, anyway. Not after the way I'd struggled trying to keep up with Cruiser earlier. Besides, it wouldn't have been as much fun without Nona along. I was worried about her. She'd had her lows before; we all do. But I'd never seen her this depressed. Not over a guy. Why did she have to go and pick someone like Medwyn to fall in love with? I would have gladly settled for the guy with the nose ring.

Chapter Twenty

Monday morning started with the usual routine around my place. Empty Cruiser. Feed Cruiser. Exercise Cruiser. Only the last step in the regimen would be more aptly described as "Exercise Beanie" by the time I was dragged at the end of a leash for a mile uphill.

I heard the phone ringing as I stumbled in the door. I made it on the last ring.

"Hello?"

"I'm glad I caught you. I was just about to hang up," Skip said.

I struggled to catch my breath.

"Beanie? You still there?"

"Whew!"

"What's up, kiddo? You sound pooped."

"I am. Just got back from exercising Cruiser."

"Sounds more like Cruiser exercised you."

"I'm still not exactly at the top of my game after those margaritas Saturday night."

"I know what you mean. Say, are you still going to attend the community powwow this evening?"

"Yeah. I'm covering it for the Times."

"I'm heading over to Tallis Headquarters this morning. Want to come along?"

"I'll be there as soon as I get cleaned up and have another cup of coffee."

"Okay, Beanie. Bye."

A quick shower and a gulp of coffee later, I headed for the front door, Cruiser's cue that we were going cruisin'. This time he didn't even blink an eye. He wasn't about to budge from his pillow for the rest of the day. He'd already had his workout, thank you very much. After our adventure in the meadow the day before, I wondered that he'd even asked for a walk this morning.

Skip's phone call hadn't wakened Nona, so I just left the two of them to snore while I went to the station to see Skip.

I drove past the amusement park and the former location of The Outdoorsman, always the high water mark for the fashion-minded sportsman or sportswoman. I bought Nona her first pair of cross-country skis there. With my parents, we skied beautiful and remote Spooner Summit, just spitting distance from the scene of the first victim of the Tahoe Terror.

I remembered what I had seen in the meadow with Cruiser. I knew snow blindness could play tricks on the eyes. So could those margaritas from the night before. If it weren't for the prints I saw and the fact Cruiser saw something that scared the fuzz off him, I'd have thought I imagined the whole thing. Cruiser and I knew it was no hallucination, but Cruiser can't talk and who would believe a woman who makes up stories for a living?

Skip sat wading through a mountain of paperwork when I arrived.

"I'm not quite ready yet, Beanie. How about some coffee before we head out?"

"Sure. I rushed the last one." I followed him into his office and sat by the window. The sun streamed through the Venetian blinds, making zebra stripes of light on the scuffed white linoleum floor. Filaments of dust scattered in the air as I leaned back and bumped the blinds. Skip returned presently, toting two cups of steaming coffee.

"Hey, don't you guys ever dust around here?" I joked.

"No, but the janitor does."

"Well, he sure isn't earning his money. He missed the blinds. Does he sweep the dirt under the carpet, too?"

"I wouldn't be too surprised. Seems to be the norm around here."

"What do you mean?"

"Oh, nothing. Just kidding."

He smiled when he said it, but when he scratched his chin in his thoughtful way, I knew he wasn't kidding at all.

"How's Nona?" Skip asked as we drove toward Tallis Headquarters. "Still upset about getting stood up the other night?"

"I suppose. She seemed kind of depressed all day yesterday. She didn't even want to go with me for our Sunday sundae."

"She'll get over it."

"Oh, I know. I've been through this kind of thing with her so many times I've lost count."

"A pretty girl like Nona should be breaking hearts, not having hers broken."

"I wouldn't worry about it. She's left a long trail of broken hearts."

"I know the feeling. I've had mine broken once or twice."

"Rita?"

"Uh, huh. How did you know?"

"I'd have to be blind, deaf, and dumb not to."

"I guess it's no secret I used to have a thing for her."

"Used to? You could have fooled me the way you were cavorting with her on the dance floor Saturday night."

"I apologize, Beanie. That wasn't very gentlemanly behavior after asking you to the dance."

"As I recall, I asked *you*."

"Oh, yeah."

"Anyway, I wasn't the only one who was offended. Stoddard wasn't too happy about you dancing with his date, either."

"So I noticed. She's probably one reason why Stoddard wants me off the force."

"And the other reasons?"

"I can't tell you any more."

"You know you can trust me, Skip."

"I know. I just can't talk about it right now, okay?"

"Yeah, sure."

I decided to drop the subject for the time being, but I began to get a bad feeling about this *menagerie* à trois. I also wondered how deeply Skip might be involved. Cruiser might have to help me dig this rabbit out of his hole.

Tallis' palace shone like an Indian head nickel in the morning sun. The unique design of the building reminded me of a one-armed bandit, which perfectly summed up their corporate strategy. They were determined to destroy my people's lands to turn a tidy profit. If it was a choice between salvaging the last vestiges of a civilization or making a quick buck, it always came down to money in the end.

Ironically, the entrance to the building mimicked the wealth of natural resources Tallis was so busily plundering. A mock aspen grove lined a man-made creek spilling from a waterfall into a fake mountain pond. Ice crusted the edges of the pond, making it look even colder than the building itself.

I was astonished by the grandeur of the lobby with its designer furniture and polished stainless steel fixtures. The receptionist's desk occupied a small island in the middle of another faux pond, filled with the largest specimens of Kokanee salmon I've ever seen. We stepped across a bridge to the desk. A harried-looking young woman tried to type between phone calls.

"Excuse me," Skip said.

"Yes?" She peered up at us through gold-framed glasses.

"We're looking for..."

"Just a moment please," she interrupted to answer another call.

Skip eyed the giant salmon in the pond like a hungry cat. He probably wished he had brought along his fishing pole.

"Now, what can I do for you?" she said.

"Could you direct us to Medwyn Abercarn's office?" Skip asked.

"Who?"

"Medwyn Abercarn," I repeated.

"Just a moment, please."

She tapped a key on the computer, then waited while the organization chart came up on the screen.

"Could you spell that for me?" she asked.

"A-B-E-R..."

"Oh, here it is."

I watched as she scrolled down to his name. I noticed Medwyn's home address also listed on the page. I filed it quickly in my memory.

"Which room is he in, Miss?" Skip queried.

"Says here, 514."

"Great, thanks." We turned to walk to the elevators.

"I'm terribly sorry," she said. "It seems there's been a mistake here."

"A mistake?" I asked.

"This chart should have been updated months ago. Mr. Abercarn no longer works here."

Skip and I exchanged glances.

The receptionist leaned forward and whispered, "Please don't mention this oversight to Mr. Brennan, okay? I'd like to keep my job."

"Don't worry, Miss, we won't," Skip assured. "By the way, where might we find Mr. Brennan?"

"I just reviewed his schedule before you came in. You can catch him at the council meeting over at Zephyr Cove Resort at 7:00 this evening."

"Thanks." I said. We turned to leave the quicksilver lobby.

As we exited the revolving door, Mike Stoddard entered the building. He locked eyes with Skip for a moment as they carouseled in the door. The expression on his face resembled that of a naughty boy who had just been caught with his fingers in the pie.

Chapter Twenty-one

"I thought you'd never get here, Beanie. Hurry, they're just about to start," Skip said. The parking lot was packed bumper to bumper. Just about everyone in South Tahoe had turned out for the Zephyr Cove showdown, just a stone's throw from Cave Rock, which had fast become a stone of contention. All the South Tahoe media were covering the event.

When we entered the main conference room, Sonseah, Dan, and the rest of the Tribal Council were seated at one end of a long table; Brennan and what remained of the ranks of Tallis' executives were seated at the other end. In the middle, literally and figuratively, was the Forest Service, represented by Terry Chambers, whose job it would be to help both factions reach a compromise over Cave Rock. The stage had been set for a confrontation. The only thing needed was war paint. I decided to rely primarily on my tape recorder. I didn't want to miss a drumbeat of this powwow.

Sonseah spoke first, looking elegantly ethnic, as usual, in her beaded deerskin.

"Cave Rock is sacred to our people. A highway already tunnels through the stone. To allow it to be further desecrated by climbers who hammer holes in it and defile it with their very presence can no longer be tolerated by our people. For 15,000 years we lived here, long before the White Man came to drive us from our land. The time has come for us to fight for what is rightfully ours. We will no longer be considered trespassers in our own domain."

Dan Silvernail added, "My parents died on the reservation with their dream of returning to the basin unfulfilled. Carson City is not our true home. It never has been. We will do whatever it takes to reclaim our ancestral lands.

We have great hopes that the Presidential Summit next summer will help us in our plight."

"Mr. Brennan, would you care to respond?" Terry asked.

Brennan shot his cuffs and adjusted his silk tie.

"We appreciate having the opportunity to speak openly about our goals for improving the Tahoe basin. As always, Tallis has the best interests of the community in mind. We believe our newest construction will boost the economy of this area, which will benefit everyone, including the Washoe. We are eager to work with the community and confident a compromise can be reached so that we can move forward with the Cave Rock Project."

"Thank you, Mr. Brennan. I see Ms. Little Feather wishes to respond. Go ahead."

"In the history of Indians and Whites, how many such *compromises* have been struck and subsequently broken?"

"Ancient history," retorted Brennan. "It has nothing to do with now."

"It has everything to do with it!" Dan Silvernail bellowed. The news cameras swiveled in his direction. "We're all victims because of you and your kind."

"You people are living in the past, Silvernail. That's why you've never successfully adapted to modern society. Try living in the twenty-first century, why don't you?" Spittle collected in the corners of Brennan's mouth as his and Dan's argument escalated.

"We were forced to adapt to life on reservations, while you stole our lands, our food, our lives!" Dan yelled, pounding his fist on the table. "We weren't permitted to share your world!"

More angry words were exchanged. Soon the whole room was in an uproar. I feared a replay of the SaveNSense Siege might be imminent.

"Gentlemen, gentlemen!" Terry broke in.

"May I interject something?" I said, rising from my seat.

"Yes, of course. This is a public forum. Anyone in the room may speak who wishes to. You have the floor, Ma'am."

"My name is Elsie MacBean, and I am Washoe, too,"
I began.

"Only half," I heard Sonseah snipe.

"Please, Ms. Little Feather. Ms. MacBean has the
floor now," Terry admonished.

"All right, half Washoe, but whatever affects them
also affects me. I know well the pain of my ancestors. My
grandfather was full-blooded Washoe. So was my mother.
However, I'm a realist, too, and we will never solely occupy
the Tahoe basin as we once did. There are too many others
who love the lake as we do. Not for the same reasons or as
gently, but the fact remains that Tahoe has become a tourist-
dependent community, and people will continue to use and,
in some cases, abuse our natural resources. We must compromise and work together to make this the best possible
environment for everyone. Washington's lawmakers may
help us in our struggle to reclaim some of our ancestral lands,
but that remains to be seen. In the meantime, we must reach
some kind of agreement over Cave Rock that meets the interests of both sides of the issue."

"Thank you, Elsie," Terry said. "I couldn't have said
it better." The room broke out in applause, all except for
Sonseah and Dan. Brennan made like Elvis and left the building.

"Bravo, Beanie!" Skip said as I sat back down.

"I just said what's needed saying for a long time."

"Order, order!" Terry said. "I'd like to propose that
we schedule another meeting next week to discuss how we
can better approach the problems we've discussed here tonight."

I noticed Dan and Sonseah put their heads together,
then Dan got up to leave just after Brennan did.

A light skiff of snow had begun to fall as we emptied out into the parking lot.

"Say, how about another dose of killer chili tomorrow night at my place, Skip?" I said. "I have a batch of it in
the freezer I can thaw out."

"I still have a ton of paperwork backlogged, but I'll
try to get caught up before then."

"Fine. Just come over when you're ready. I'll have
the chili on the stove and a Bud in the fridge. You're off

duty by 6:00, right?"

"Should be."

"Perfect. We can kick back and chew the fat about the case. I need to get some more details."

"Sure thing, Beanie. See you then."

As I walked across the parking lot to my car, I noticed Dan Silvernail following Brennan to his BMW. A moment later Silvernail caught up and grabbed the sleeve of Brennan's tailored jacket. Under the parking lot lights, I could see the two men arguing. It was the last time I would see Richard Brennan alive.

Chapter Twenty-two

I decided to break with my usual Tuesday breakfast ritual at Debbie's Diner and opted for International House of Pancakes instead. I felt like a short stack of pancakes, but I didn't care to see a certain short, stacked waitress named Rita Ramirez, especially after the other night at the casino. I stopped briefly at the Times to drop off a diskette on the Zephyr Cove meeting for Carla.

As I drove east, the lake was a stunning winterscape in hues of powder blue at the shoreline, to cyan, to indigo at its deepest point. No motorboats or jet skis marred her glassy surface; no sunbathers splashed on her shores and littered her beaches, which were deserted except for a few people exercising their dogs. In fact, the streets were pretty much deserted, too. I had begun to notice people walking in pairs at night, if they ventured out at all after dark. The tension in this community had grown palpable, especially after the fourth body turned up.

I never made it to IHOP. As I drove past Debbie's, I spotted the pulsing blue and red lights of police cars, television reporters, and a crowd gathered around the west side of the restaurant. I saw Skip trying unsuccessfully to cordon off the scene with yellow tape. I pulled into the parking lot to see what the commotion was about, but I think I already knew. The Terror had claimed yet another victim.

"Am I glad to see you," Skip said as I skip-roped the yellow tape he attached to a nearby tree.

"Jeez, I don't believe this. Not another one?"

"'Fraid so. We got a call from the manager of the restaurant about twenty minutes ago."

"Who is it this time?"

"Richard Brennan."

"Brennan? But he was fine last night at 9:00."

"Well, he isn't fine now," Skip said.

The entire population of South Lake Tahoe seemed to be milling around in the parking lot.

"Word travels fast, I see."

"Like a Concorde with a tail wind."

"Where is he?" I asked.

"In there," Skip said, pointing to the dumpster.

I lifted the lid and looked inside. It clanged shut when I gasped and let go. "Brennan isn't looking his usual natty self."

"So I noticed."

"He was always dressed to kill, but I never expected..."

"At least we have a witness this time," Skip interrupted.

"Who?"

"Rita."

"Has she made a positive ID?"

"Better go ask the boss about that."

I saw Stoddard puffing on a cigarette stub as he scribbled in his notebook. His sunglasses couldn't conceal the ugly bruise over his left eye. I pulled out my own note pad and pen as I approached him. Stoddard's posture stiffened.

"Sheriff Stoddard, got a minute?"

He didn't look up. "What for?"

"Mind answering a couple of questions?"

He chewed on his coffin nail and kept on writing. I didn't wait for a response I probably wasn't going to get.

"Deputy Cassidy tells me you have a witness to this murder."

"Sure do."

"Would that be Rita Ramirez?"

"Uh, huh. Said she saw someone hanging around the dumpster as she came off her shift last night."

"Has she made a positive identification, yet?"

"No, but she will as soon as we organize a lineup."

"Could she describe the suspect?"

"She said he was tall with long hair pulled back in a

ponytail. I can think of only one person offhand who hated Brennan enough to kill him and who also wears his hair that way."

"Who, Sheriff?"

"Dan Silvernail, of course. You'll have to excuse me. I see I need to supervise these guys before they bungle this investigation."

"Of course." I watched Stoddard crush out his cigarette under his boot and march over to the dumpster where Skip worked over Brennan's body. I stashed my pen and notebook in my purse and followed him. I didn't want to miss anything important.

"Be sure to bag the hands, Hop...Er...Cassidy," Stoddard said, his tone subdued. "The murderer may have left some evidence under the fingernails."

"Whatever you say, Bigfoot," I heard Skip mumble as Stoddard walked away.

I watched Skip as he placed a paper sack around each of Brennan's hands and secured them at the wrists with tape, a gruesome task made commonplace by an item you would use to carry home a loaf of bread or a quart of milk. Except in this case, when the grocery bagger asked you, "Paper or plastic?" you always answered "paper." Using plastic bags would cause premature spoiling.

I studied Skip's face as he worked over the body. His jaw muscles twitched like he had a mouthful of Mexican jumping beans. I knew he tried his best not to show his emotions, whether it was over troublesome co-workers or corpses. Suddenly, I felt tremendous admiration for him, or maybe it was a bit more than that. He must have sensed me studying him, because he began to make idle conversation as he worked.

"Where were you headed, anyway?"

"I was going to IHOP for breakfast, but I seem to have lost my appetite."

"Not me." He scraped a tissue sample from the victim's throat wound.

I swallowed hard when I felt my gorge rising. "Jeez, you never do."

"Is that invitation for tonight still good?"

"You have a standing invitation for my chili, Skip.

You know that."

"Don't forget the onions, and the cold beer."

"Chili and a chilly brew. Got it."

"See you later."

"You can fill me in then."

"Natch."

When I came in my front door, I found Nona kneeling in a corner of the living room holding a wad of paper towels.

"Some house-trained dog you've got here, Mom. Just look what he did to your floor!"

"Cruiser, shame on you. Naughty boy!"

Cruiser cowered and gave me a sheepish look that said, *Sorry, Mom. Couldn't help it.* I took pity, sat down on the couch, and called him over to me. He slinked to my side and plopped his chin on my knee, looking up into my eyes for forgiveness. He got it. He knew he had me wrapped around his dewclaw. Petting Cruiser was good medicine. My nerves were on edge after what I'd seen in the dumpster. Everyone's nerves were on edge. Someone had to find the killer, and soon. From the looks of things, Stoddard and his boys weren't going to pin the tail on The Terror any time soon.

"It's okay, boy. I'll let it go this time, but just in case, maybe we'd better have another lesson with the doggy door. Can you handle the cleanup in here, Auntie Nona?"

"Honestly, Mom. Sometimes you're downright sickening when it comes to that dog. And speaking of sickening..." Nona frowned and crinkled her nose.

"Come on, Cruiser. Potty time." Cruiser's toenails clicked on the kitchen floor as he followed me to the back door.

"Well, no wonder you went potty in the house. Your door is locked." I unlatched the security panel, laying it to one side, then stepped outside the kitchen door and closed it behind me. We'd have to go through the motions again, just to be sure there were no more lapses in house training.

When I knelt down with another Beggin' Strip to coax Cruiser through the door, I saw deep furrows cut in the wood of the kitchen door. They looked like...claw marks!

Something *had* been trying to get inside. No wonder Cruiser hadn't been his usual easygoing self lately. I began to get the definite feeling we were being stalked, and it wasn't a good feeling.

"Nona, did you lock Cruiser's door last night? I was sure I left it unlocked when we went to bed."

"Yes, I locked it."

"Then how did Cruiser get out this morning? He didn't wake me up like he usually does."

"When he couldn't raise you, he woke me up instead. I let him out the back door to do his business, then went back to bed."

"Why did you lock the door?"

"I heard noises again last night. It spooked me. After the other night, I felt nervous about leaving the dog door unlocked. You never know what might try to come through there."

"Well, better safe than sorry, I guess."

"Speaking of guessing, bet you can't guess who called just before you came in."

"Skip?"

"No. Guess again."

"Carla?"

"Nope."

"Agatha Christie's crumpets! I don't know. Who?"

"Medwyn!"

"What did *he* want?"

"A date."

"After standing you up?"

"Oh, he explained that to me."

"Well, perhaps he'd like to explain his behavior to me, too. I don't like seeing you hurt."

"He said it was strictly business."

"I think he's giving *you* the business, Nona."

"You're being unfair, Mom. We both just jumped to the wrong conclusion."

"I don't think there are any wrong conclusions to jump to with Medwyn. I just don't trust this guy."

"You say that about everyone I date."

"No, I don't."

"Do, so."

"Do not."

Cruiser came dashing back through the dog door when he heard loud voices. We both fell silent, but the silence didn't last long.

"So you're going to see him again?" I prodded, not wanting to hear the answer I would get.

"He deserves a second chance."

"I wish you'd reconsider, Nonie." I gave her my best abandoned basset look.

"I'm a big girl now, remember?"

The only way I could keep Nona from seeing Medwyn again was to lock her in her room. And then she'd probably just crawl out the window like she did as a teenager when I disapproved of her dates. I was licked, and I knew it, and so did Cruiser, who was busy licking my hand to try and calm me down.

I sighed. "Like you said, you're old enough to make your own decisions, and your own mistakes. I just hope you're not making a big one with him."

"Don't worry, Mom. I'm not."

"Where's he taking you, anyway?"

"To The Colosseum to see Mr. Mysterioso."

Great, a magician! Maybe *he* can make this Medwyn character disappear. And how about the Tahoe Terror, while he's at it?

"He said he has something important to ask me, Mom."

I felt my stomach plummet to my toes. "What?"

"I don't know, but I think he might be about to pop the question."

"You don't mean..."

"I'm pretty sure he's going to ask me to marry him."

"Don't be ridiculous. You can't marry Medwyn, Nona."

"Why not?" Nona hooked her hands on her hips, her face clouding up.

"You don't know anything about him, that's why."

"I know all I need to know."

"Please think carefully about this before you commit yourself to anything, dear. I don't want you to make a mistake you'll regret for the rest of your life."

"But that's just the point, isn't it, Mom?"

"What do you mean?"

"It *is* my life!"

I sighed, my defeat assured in this battle of Baby Boomer vs. Generation X. "I'm only going to say one more thing, Nona."

Nona rolled her eyes. "What, Mother?"

"Promise me you'll be careful tonight, okay? Something evil is stalking this community. I don't want you to be the next victim of the Tahoe Terror." I brushed Nona's long, soft hair away from her pretty face.

Nona smiled at me, her ginger spice eyes exuding patronizing patience for her foolish old mother. "You raised me, Mom. Have a little faith in me, okay?" I hated to admit it, but she had a valid point.

Chapter Twenty-three

At quarter to six the doorbell rang. I went to answer the door. It was Skip.

"All right, Beanie, I'm here. You can bring on that hot chili and cold beer."

"Come in. The chili'll be ready in a jiffy."

"Great. How 'bout a chilly beer while I wait?"

"Make yourself comfortable on the couch with your fur friend over there. I'll go get you one."

Skip took a seat next to Cruiser, who thumped his tail twice in greeting, then resumed his nap.

I went to the fridge and tossed a can of beer to Nona. "Give this to Skip, will you? I've gotta get this chili defrosted in a hurry. Sure wish I had a microwave oven. I should have already had this thawed out, but we got kind of sidetracked, didn't we?"

"Not my fault, Mom," Nona said, juggling the ice-cold beer can from hand to hand as she headed for the door.

The chili had just started to melt in the pan, so I grabbed myself a brewskie and went into the living room to chat with Skip and Nona.

"Mom, Skip was just telling me they've collared a suspect in these murders."

"I thought you seemed pretty chipper, Skipper," I said. "What's going on?"

"Stoddard says we've definitely got our man."

"Who?"

"Dan Silvernail." Rita made a positive ID in the lineup. Arraignment is pending."

"Boy, Stoddard's not letting the grass grow under his boots on this one, is he?"

"See, Mom? I told you that you were way off base

about Medwyn."

Skip scratched his chin. "What about Medwyn?"

"Mom's such a worry wart, I think she was even beginning to suspect Medwyn."

"All I know is there have been some pretty bizarre goings-on around here lately, and it all seemed to start about the time you started dating Medwyn."

"That's just a coincidence," Nona said.

"I think you've read one too many Sherlock Holmes mysteries, Beanie."

"Yeah, Mom. Next you'll be telling us it's the Hound of the Baskervilles." Nona and Skip made howling sounds. Cruiser sat upright and joined in the howlfest. Nona and Skip broke into gales of laughter.

"It's no laughing matter, you two. People are dying out there. God only knows who'll be next."

The room went silent as a stone. A gravestone.

"Well, you're right about one thing at least," Skip said.

"What?"

"These are unlike any murders we've ever seen before."

"Come clean, Skip. There's definitely something you're not telling me."

Nona yawned. "Mind if I log onto the Internet for awhile, Mom?"

"No, go ahead." Nona went into my office and shut the door.

"Just as well," Skip said. "I didn't really want her hearing the details of the case, anyway."

"Me, neither. Now, what's going on?"

"As I see it, all signs point to Silvernail."

"How can you be sure?"

"Brennan wasn't killed by an animal."

"I know."

"How could you?"

"I was at the scene, remember? I saw the wounds on Brennan's throat. Anyone could see at a glance they were nothing like the wounds inflicted on the other victims."

"Very astute of you, Beanie."

"His throat was cut with a sharp instrument, a knife

most likely. And he was killed someplace else. There was very little blood in the dumpster."

"The body was dumped after the murder, all right."

"I'm guessing the amylase test came up negative, too?"

"Right again."

"There's still no proof it was Silvernail, though."

"Well, he always carries that Redskin tomahawk of his."

I scowled at his remark. "That's reserved for scalp-ing   politically   incorrect   deputies,   Skip."

"Sorry. It's just that everyone is eager to see the end of these killings."

"Surely not enough to accuse a man of murder just because his skin is the wrong color."

"The Sheriff seems certain Silvernail's the perp," Skip said.

"Now that I think of it, this kind of publicity could really hurt his chances for election."

"No kidding. Nobody feels safe on the streets here any more, and Tallis is screaming bloody murder."

"Must be why we saw Stoddard over at Headquar-ters. Tallis seems to carry a lot a weight with him."

"What d'ya mean?" Skip asked.

"Think about it. He can pull a lot of strings for Tallis if he's elected. And the sooner this case is wrapped up, the sooner Tallis makes money from all the tourists coming to Cave Rock Resort."

"I don't quite follow you, Beanie."

"I haven't pieced this whole puzzle together yet, but it's my opinion Stoddard would sell his own mother into slavery to get elected."

"And everyone else, too."

"What do you mean?"

Skip didn't answer. His silence gave me all the an-swer I needed.

"Listen, Skip. I know you want to do the right thing, even if it might cost you your job."

Skip nodded. "What I care most about is that the people in this community are safe from harm."

"Which makes you a better cop than Stoddard ever

could be," I said, patting his arm.

Skip's face flushed redder than my chili sauce. "Thanks, Beanie."

"We can't let your boss sweep this case under the rug and conveniently pin it on Silvernail."

"What makes you so certain Silvernail's not the killer? You saw how he and Brennan got into it at the meeting."

"Yeah, I know. I saw them arguing later in the parking lot, too."

"Then what more proof do you need?"

"I just have this hunch there's something more to this. You've convinced me of that much."

"How'd I do that?"

"C'mon. I know you better than your own mother. When you clam up, there's a darn good reason."

Skip scratched his chin. I knew he was cracking.

"All right. I'm busted, but if I tell you what I know, you can't tell another soul. I'll lose my job for sure, if you do."

"Agreed."

"Okay. I have it on good authority Stoddard may be involved in some kind of illegal activity."

"What kind?"

"Dog fighting."

"You heard about that, too?"

"Yeah, how'd you find out about it?"

"While researching an article I wrote for Fur and Feather Quarterly. How did *you*?"

"I got wind of it." Apparently he wasn't planning to report from whence this ill wind blew.

"Why didn't you report it, Skip? That's the worst kind of animal abuse."

"You're the big animal rights activist. Why didn't you?"

"I did. The Tahoe Humane Society is investigating it, but these dogfight ring creeps are pretty sneaky operators. It's hard to catch them in the act unless you go undercover. It may come to that."

"Say, don't I smell something burning?" Skip made Cruiser-style sniffing motions at the air.

"You're just trying to throw me off the track."

"I'd say you'd better make tracks toward the kitchen. I really do smell something burning, Beanie."

When I saw Cruiser sniffing the air, too, I knew Skip wasn't kidding. "Good grief! I forgot all about the chili."

I scurried to the kitchen with Cruiser right behind me. Perhaps the smell of the smoking chili had sparked his appetite. In a moment, I heard the crunch of kibble. I felt relieved he had begun eating again. He'd seemed kind of depressed lately. There's nothing more dismal looking than a down-in-the-mouth basset hound. Nona and Skip appeared at the kitchen door to find me holding a smoking saucepan with a clump of charred chili at the bottom.

"Sorry, guys. Looks like you're out of luck for dinner, unless you like Cajun blackened chili."

"Forget it," Skip said. "I have an idea. How about if I take you two to the Fifties Drive-in tonight? My treat, for a change."

"Hey, sounds good. I've always intended to try it. But they don't serve vegetarian, do they?"

"I'm sure there's something meatless on the menu. I know they have chocolate milk shakes and French fries; there's no meat in those."

"Now you're talking. Last one in the car is a fat basset."

Cruiser followed us at warp speed, which of course is only a waddle for a fat basset.

Chapter Twenty-four

The Marcels were bomp-pa-pa-bomping "Blue Moon" as Skip scarfed down the artery-clogger special, a double cheeseburger with extra mayo and French fries to die for, literally. As we sat bundled up in Skip's 4x4 at the Fifties Drive-In, snow collected on the windshield even though we were sheltered under a tin roof. Yeah, we could have gone inside where it was warm, but it just wouldn't have been the same. Instead, I turned up the collar of my jacket, pulled the flaps of my deerstalker down over my ears, and dug in. Nona and I ordered thick chocolate shakes. I broke down and ordered French fries, too. Cruiser whined and begged in the back of the car, so occasionally I lobbed a fry over my shoulder. Like a toad catching flies, he snapped up each one in midair.

"This is fun, Skip," I said as I slurped the last of my shake and pitched the last fry to home base, Cruiser's mouth.

"Yeah, thanks for the treat," Nona said. "Mom really digs this Fifties stuff. She's expecting the Second Coming of Elvis any day."

"Cool it, Spice Girl." I gave Nona a playful noogie on her noggin.

The static crackle of the police radio cut through our banter. I tried to make out the conversation, but Skip may as well have been ordering a double bacon cheeseburger from a Jack-in-the-Box drive-thru.

"Can you translate that?" I said.

"Stoddard's in Barton Memorial Hospital."

"Why?"

"Sounds like he's been attacked."

"What happened?"

"I couldn't hear that part too clearly. I guess I'd

better drop you gals off now and go check it out."

"No way," I said. "I'm not about to miss this."

"Can I come, too?" Nona asked.

"Better not, honey."

"Aw, come on, Mom."

"What part of NO don't you understand, NO-na?"

Nona huffed and crossed her arms.

"Besides, Cruiser needs his exercise after all those French fries."

"Very funny, Mother."

After we dropped off our passengers, Skip and I made our way back to the emergency room. The facility seemed quiet, except for one room, where we saw a flurry of activity. It didn't take us three guesses to figure out the location of our impatient patient.

When we stepped into the cubicle, Stoddard looked whiter than the sheet tucked around him. The doctor worked on his right arm, which had been badly slashed, as was his neck.

"You were lucky, Sheriff. This came within a centimeter of your jugular. What kind of animal did you say it was?"

"Couldn't tell. Might have been a bear. It all happened so fast, and it was dark."

"Don't bears hibernate in the winter?"

"Not this one," Stoddard said, wincing as the doctor examined the wound.

"Doctor, better save a sample of any saliva or foreign tissue in the wound for the crime lab," Skip said.

Stoddard shot Skip a look I was glad he didn't see. I was also glad he had taken the upper hand. His boss probably couldn't be trusted with any evidence related to this case.

"Sure, I'll have Staff prepare some slides," the doctor said.

"Thanks, Doc."

"I'll be right back, then we'll finish getting you patched up, Sheriff."

The doctor left us alone with Stoddard.

"Why don't you tell us exactly what happened," I

said. I expected Stoddard to order me out of the room, but he didn't.

"I...It came from out of nowhere," he stammered. He suddenly seemed scared and vulnerable, a new look for him.

"What do you mean?" Skip asked.

"It was the most hideous thing I ever saw. Huge fangs and glaring eyes, and it made the most awful sound. I turned and ran as fast as I could, but it overtook me like I was standing still, breathing down my neck like some kind of demon from hell. I tell you it was determined to take me out."

"You say you think it was a bear?" I asked.

"I honestly can't say for sure. Like I said, it was dark and I couldn't see. At one point I thought it might be a dog, but it was much too large."

Skip and I exchanged glances.

"All I know is it was terrifying. It was kind of shimmery." Stoddard jabbered like a madman. I'd never seen anyone so scared.

"You mean phosphorescent?" I asked, mostly for Skip's benefit. I'd already seen what Stoddard had with my own eyes.

"Yeah, like one of those kids glow-in-the-dark toys."

"Huh?" Skip looked understandably puzzled by his boss's description. He shot me another look I loosely translated as *This guy's Cheese Whiz has slid off his cracker*. I, on the other hand, knew that for perhaps the first time in his corrupt life, Stoddard was telling the truth.

The doctor stepped back into the cubicle. "Well, let's finish getting you fixed up."

"Then can I leave?" Stoddard asked.

"No, we'd better keep you here overnight for observation, and we'll have to start a rabies series."

"Rabies?" Stoddard paled even more.

"Just a standard precaution in a case like this, Sheriff. We wouldn't want you to start foaming at the mouth."

Skip's mouth worked as he tried his best not to laugh at the doctor's comment. He'd seen Stoddard foam at the mouth plenty of times around the office.

"I think I'd better go home and check on Nona and

Cruiser, Skip."

    "Sure, Beanie."

    "Oh, Officer, just a minute."

    "Yes, doctor?"

    "Don't forget your slides."

    "Mind if I drop this off at the lab on the way back, Beanie? It won't take a minute."

    "You bet."

    I felt relieved when Nona met us at the front door. Cruiser hadn't budged from his pillow on the couch. If Tom had a watchdog in mind when he brought Cruiser home, he should have rescued a stray rottweiler, instead of a basset.

    "Want some cocoa before you head back out, Skip?"

    "No, but I'll take you up on some coffee. Something tells me I won't be getting much sleep tonight."

    "Me, neither. I've got a little story spinning to do later."

    "I'll stoke up the fire while you brew the coffee."

    When I returned with cocoa and coffee, Skip sat next to Cruiser on the couch in front of the fire. Nona had said her good-nights and went to curl up with some magazines. It might have been almost romantic, just the two of us there in the flickering firelight, if it weren't for a certain hound dog snoring away between us and the undeniable fact that Skip and I were just good friends. Mind you, Tom and I started out as friends, too. He almost threw me with his next question.

    "Think we're getting any closer, Beanie?"

    "Huh?" I felt my face flush, or maybe it was just the fire. Or another hot flash.

    "On solving the case."

    "Oh."

    I sipped my cocoa, staring into the flames as I mulled over the incidents of the past week. When I opened my mouth to speak, Skip started to laugh.

    "What's so funny?"

    "You are," he said, pulling out his hanky. He reached over and wiped away my whipped cream mustache.

    I laughed. "Thanks."

"Do you believe Stoddard's story?" Skip said.

"Yes. I take it you don't, though."

"I'm not sure. My opinion is, I think this investigation's sent him off the deep end. Or he's hitting the bottle pretty hard. You remember how he acted at the casino? Not exactly behavior becoming an officer and candidate for mayor."

"You may have something there, all right, but I believe he's telling the truth. You saw him at the hospital. He was scared stiff by something out there."

"True. But he's nuts, Beanie. Has to be."

"Not necessarily. Like I told you before, I've been seeing some pretty strange things myself around here lately."

"Yeah, I know. The thing at your window."

"Listen, Skip. I didn't tell you this before, because I knew you wouldn't believe me. I saw something else weird that night."

"What now?"

"Pretty much the same thing Stoddard told us earlier."

Skip picked up my empty cup and peered inside. "What was in that cocoa, anyway?"

I snatched it back. "I'm serious."

"I know. That's what worries me."

"You know how he described a shimmering effect?"

"Uh, huh."

"I know this sounds bizarre, but it's a perfect description of what I saw."

"So now the killer is Casper, the not-so-friendly ghost? Maybe it's time you took a long vacation with that money you won."

"But there have been other strange things, Skip."

"Like what?"

"Well, the missing shoes, for instance. You told me yourself that during the search of each victim's house, a shoe mate was missing."

"True."

"And the iridescent powder I found on my dress at the dance, remember?"

"Oh, yeah."

"I thought it was just dirt or dust, until I discovered

the same thing on Cruiser. He probably brushed against the door frame. It must have rubbed off of whatever was trying to get through his dog door."

"So you're saying the killer is a ghost with a shoe fetish? Man, this is getting stranger by the minute, Beanie." Skip hummed the theme from "The Twilight Zone."

"Not so strange to me. The Washoe believe spirit beings can inflict bodily harm on others."

"But ghosts with designer shoes? You've watched one too many episodes of 'The X-files'."

"Can you be serious for just a minute, Skip?"

"Okay, okay." He took another sip of coffee.

"These ancient legends survive for good reason. Something evil has fallen upon this valley."

"But...come on. Spooks? I still say Stoddard was attacked by some kind of animal. We already have the murderer locked up in the slammer."

"I admit your theory sounds more plausible." I downed the last of my cocoa.

"Of course it does. There's a landslide of evidence pointing to Silvernail being the killer. It's well known he despised Tallis, and Brennan most of all. Why wouldn't he want to destroy the company?"

I had to admit that Dan Silvernail seemed to be the obvious choice for this murder rap. He was the right color, anyway. I still wasn't convinced, though. There were just too many pieces of this puzzle that didn't quite fit. For all we knew, there might be more than one killer stalking Tahoe. Terror times two.

Chapter Twenty-five

I was awakened the next morning by a crash in the living room. Cruiser was out the bedroom door quicker than a jackrabbit in a harem, with me hot on his tail.

"What happened?" I saw Nona collecting the pieces of her special cocoa cup from the floor.

"Everything's fine, Mom. Skip startled me. I didn't know he was still here." We were all getting a little jumpy.

"It was so late by the time we finished talking, I just invited him to sleep on the couch for the night. How was the couch, by the way?"

"Very comfortable. No wonder Cruiser likes it so much."

"I'll make us some breakfast. Use the shower if you want, Skip."

"Thanks, I will."

"Maybe after breakfast, we can take Cruiser for his walk."

"I'd like to stay, but I'd better get going. They'll be sending out the *SWAT* team for me if I'm late this morning."

An hour later the phone rang.

"Skip, you just left here. What's up?"

"We're about to question Silvernail. I knew you'd want to be here."

"I'll be right there!"

I slammed down the phone, tucked Cruiser's blanket around him and was out the door.

I wasn't prepared for what I saw when I drove up to the station. It was like the scene from the old Frankenstein movie where the villagers storm the castle with torches and pitchforks. A group of Washoe, led by none other than Sonseah, was gathered at the entrance, chanting protests against Dan Silvernail's arrest. Television reporters shouted their questions above the din. I wasn't about to plow my way through that rabble, so I slipped in the back door to Skip's office.

"Say, Skip, looks like the natives are a little restless."

"A little?"

"Things could get ugly out there if Silvernail is charged with murder."

"Yeah, I know. But Tallis is crying, 'Off with his head!' I hate being stuck in the middle of this, Beanie."

"Well, better brace yourself. I'm afraid things are coming to a head between Tallis and the Washoe, and from the looks of it, I'd say that pimple is just about to pop."

Skip made a face at my icky analogy and led me through the County Government Center to the jail. I followed him to a small room with a table and three chairs. A tape recorder was set up in the center of the table.

"Have a seat here, Beanie. I'll be right back."

Presently, Skip and another officer escorted Silvernail into the room. His brown hair hung loose around his shoulders instead of in the usual ponytail. He looked different in jail attire than in his Stetson and leather vest, but no less proud.

"Have a seat," the officer instructed.

Silvernail sat down, his eyes sparking with hatred as he studied us from across the table.

"We have some questions to ask you," Skip said.

"Not without a lawyer, you don't," Silvernail retorted.

"Give Nick Delano a buzz, will you?" Skip instructed the other officer.

"I think he's in court today."

"No, I just saw him over in the County Clerk's office."

A few minutes later, the defense attorney stepped into the room.

"Mr. Silvernail, I'm Nick Delano," the attorney said. "I'll be representing you during the questioning. Perhaps you would like to consult with me for a moment before proceeding."

Silvernail nodded.

"We'll step out of the room," Skip said.

Fifteen minutes and a cup of coffee later, we were again seated at the table across from Silvernail, accompanied this time by the public defender. Skip switched on the tape recorder and stated the date, time, and those present.

"Mr. Silvernail, we'll be asking you some questions regarding your whereabouts on the night of Richard Brennan's murder. Be advised that anything you say can and will be held against you in a court of law. Do you understand?"

Silvernail nodded.

"Please answer aloud for the tape recorder."

"Yes."

"Can you describe your whereabouts the night of Monday, November 30, after you left the meeting at Zephyr Cove?"

"Went to my girlfriend's place," Silvernail mumbled.

"Please speak directly into the microphone," Skip said.

"MY GIRLFRIENDS PLACE!" he repeated, kissing the mike.

"Back up a little bit, Mr. Silvernail. Just speak clearly in a normal tone of voice," Skip instructed. "Did anything happen immediately prior to that?"

"Yes."

"What happened?"

"I had an argument with Richard Brennan."

"About what?"

"The Cave Rock Project."

"Please explain."

"I tried to make him see our point of view on the issue," Silvernail said.

"Whose point of view?"

"The Tribal Council's."

"Did you at any time strike Richard Brennan or harm him in any way?"

"No. I never touched him. I swear."

"What happened then?"

"I stopped over at my girlfriend's."

"What time was that?"

"About 9:30."

"And what time did you leave her house?"

"Around 10:00, maybe quarter after."

"Did you go anywhere near Debbie's Diner at any time that night?"

"No! Absolutely not."

"Mind if I ask a question, Skip?" I said.

"Go ahead."

"Dan, did you see anyone else with Brennan in the Zephyr Cove Resort parking lot?"

Silvernail thought a moment.

"Yes, someone else came up to talk to him just after I walked away."

"Did you recognize the person with Brennan?"

I saw Dan's eyes lock on the **Elect Mike Stoddard for Mayor** campaign poster on the bulletin board in the hallway. "It was him!"

"Think he's telling the truth?" Skip asked as we walked back to his office.

"Yes, but thousands wouldn't."

"Brennan's time of death has been established at sometime between 10:00 P.M. and midnight. I say Silvernail's definitely our man."

"There's no denying that it's going to be virtually impossible to charge a white man with these crimes when a red man's already been implicated, but Stoddard ought to be questioned, too, Skip. Maybe you should hook him up to a lie detector."

"You don't think *he* killed Brennan? Silvernail's just trying to throw us off the trail."

"There's only one way to find out for sure."

"I seriously doubt if Stoddard will submit to a lie detector test."

"He may have to, Skip, if we're ever going to get to the bottom of all this. We should leave no stone unturned in this investigation. No one is above suspicion until the real killer is behind bars."

"All right. I'll hook him up, just as soon as he's out

of the hospital."

     "Good. After all, what do you have to lose?"

     "Only my job."

Chapter Twenty-six

"Bummer!" Nona said, examining the run in her nylons. "Mom, do you have an extra pair of pantyhose? I just put a fingernail through these."

"I'm sure I do, but they'll be too big for a bean pole like you."

"I'll just roll 'em up at the waist to take up the slack."

"Gee, thanks a heap."

"Hey, you threw the first stone when you called me a bean pole."

"Touché." I rustled through the dresser drawers until I found a pair of new taupe L'eggs still in the white plastic ovum. "Here, catch!" I said lobbing the egg across the bed like a miniature football. Nona cracked the shell open and unrolled the pantyhose. This time she carefully inched her thumbs down to the toes, the nylon appendages bunching in her hands. When she finally tugged them up, the waistline came nearly to her neck.

"Jeez, these are huge on me," she said, looking at herself in the mirror.

"Wait until you're in your forties, honey. If I know beans about Mendel's peas, those should be a perfect fit by then."

"Well, they'll have to do for now. Medwyn should be here pretty soon. How do I look?"

"Cold." I glanced at Nona's micro mini. Déjà vu! "It's winter out there, you know."

"I'll be fine."

"Better take your long down coat, dear."

Nona's eyes rolled with her impatient *Oh, Mother, pa-leeze* look. "Whatever you say, Mom."

I was chopping broccoli for a vegetable stir-fry when I heard a knock at the front door. "Mom, can you get that?" Nona called from the bathroom. I set down the knife, wiped my hands on my apron, and hurried to the door. Cruiser woke from his slumber and watched with interest.

When I opened the door, there stood the Young and the Tactless, Medwyn Abercarn.

"Nona's almost ready. Come in and have a seat," I said as we exchanged forced smiles. "Better sit in the chair over there, though. Wouldn't want Cruiser to soil that nice tux."

"Thanks for the warning," Medwyn said, eyeing Cruiser, who eyed him right back. I thought I heard Cruiser growl as he jumped down and moseyed to my bedroom. I felt like growling, too, as Medwyn sat down in Tom's easy chair.

"Nona missed you at the dance last Saturday, Medwyn."

"Excuse me?"

"The dance, remember? You two had a date."

"Oh, yes. I had a business meeting to attend and had to cancel at the last minute. I explained to Nona. She understood."

"Did she?"

"Why shouldn't she? It's the truth."

"My daughter wouldn't know the truth if it walked up and bit her right on the..."

"Ms. MacBean," Medwyn interrupted. "What is it exactly you have against me, anyway?"

Did he want the unabridged version?

"All right. For starters, I'd like to know more about your association with Tallis."

"Sure. What do you want to know?" Medwyn tapped his fingers on the chair arm.

"What's your connection with them, exactly?"

"I think I told you before. I'm a liaison for Tallis and other organizations involved in the Cave Rock Project."

"Don't you mean 'were'?"

"I don't follow you."

"No need to pretend with me, Medwyn. I know you don't work for Tallis any more."

"You've obviously been misinformed."

I wasn't giving up so easily this time. "Tell me, Medwyn. Is Tallis buying votes to further their ambitions for Tahoe?"

"They were backing Stoddard in the next election, if that's what you mean."

"Were? You mean they're not backing him any more?"

"Well, you'd really have to speak to Richard Brennan about that."

"I would, except it seems he's kind of...dead."

"Is he?" said Medwyn. His tone turned so cold I expected to see ice cubes spill from his lips. You'd have thought I'd just given the weather report: *Flash! Snow deepens tonight at MacBean cabin.*

"You haven't been reading the papers, I guess."

"I'm pretty busy these days. There's something I should tell you, Ms. MacBean. It's about Nona and me."

I couldn't speak. I waited for the other shoe to drop. And it did.

"I think I'm in love with your daughter."

"You *think*? Either you are or you aren't. Which is it?"

"I am in love with her. In fact, I'm going to ask her to marry me."

"She told me you might be working up to that."

"Then you think she'll say yes?"

"You'll have to ask Nona." I cringed at the thought of what her answer would probably be.

Medwyn's eyes glittered like pyrite in a streambed. "I'd like your blessing before I ask her tonight."

"Well, I'm afraid I can't do that."

"Why not?"

"Because you're not the right man for my daughter, that's why."

"When did you decide that?"

"The minute I laid eyes on you." And Cruiser laid teeth on him.

"Well, Mother MacBean, why don't we let Nona be the judge."

Mother MacBean?! Is that what he was planning to

call me if I became his mother-in-law? This just wouldn't do. If I hadn't already decided long ago, I knew right then and there that this man would never marry Nona if I could help it.

"Well, I think I'll go check on Nona," I said.

"Yes, it *is* getting pretty late."

This conversation with Medwyn was finito. If only I could persuade Nona to be finished with him, too.

On the way to the bedroom, I knocked on Nona's bedroom door. I wished I could lock her in, tie her up, anything to keep her from going out with Medwyn again, but it would do no good. I had to accept the fact that Nona would just have to make up her own mind about this character.

"For Heaven's sake, what's taking you so long?"

"I can't find my other shoe. Have you seen it?" Nona asked, limping one-shoed around the room.

"Did you check under the bed?"

"Yes. It's not there."

"We seem to be having a rash of shoe theft around here lately." I thought of Caruso's missing Ferragamo loafer and my own missing red pump. What could it mean?

"Better talk to that dog of yours, then. These were $200 shoes." Nona slipped into her other heels, checked her look in the mirror, and huffed out of the room to greet Medwyn.

When I went in to check on Cruiser, he was trying to climb up on my bed. I spread out his special "raining cats and dogs" quilt to protect my bedspread and gave him a boost. He curled up on the quilt and gave me a grateful lick on the hand before tucking nose to tail for a snooze. "Sweet dreams, fella," I said, stroking his head.

When I returned to the living room, Medwyn was helping Nona into her coat. Standing there at the door, he in his tux and she in her white micro mini, they looked like Mod Barbie and Ken's wedding. Medwyn and Nona married? What a horrid thought!

"It's 7:45, Nona," Medwyn said. "We'd best not keep Mr. Mysterioso waiting."

I wished I had some trick I could pull out of my hat to keep her from going with Medwyn. "Don't stay out too late," I said. "Remember, honey, you have to head back to

San Francisco tomorrow morning." I had hoped she'd spend her last evening in Tahoe with me and Cruiser. As always, Nona had a mind of her own. Couldn't imagine where she got that!

"We won't." As Nona took Medwyn's hand and pulled him toward the door, he winced. "Gee, I'm sorry. Did I hurt you?" said Nona.

He shook his head. Then I noticed the bandage on his wrist peeking from under the cuff of his sleeve.

"Oh, dear," Nona said, examining Medwyn's owie. "You're hurt."

"It's nothing. I cut myself."

I hugged Nona hard. "Be careful out there tonight, honey," I whispered in her ear. "Got your cellular?"

"Uh, huh." Nona seemed startled by my firm embrace. She looked into my eyes, and I noticed her brows knit together, the ginger sparks in her eyes fading. Just like her father, she could always read me like a book. As she followed her own Mr. Mysterioso out the door into the snow flurries, I knew what she saw in my eyes. Fear. Fear as numbing as the icicles gripping the eaves of my cabin in their sharp, frozen fangs. I feared mostly for Nona, for I knew that somewhere out in the stormy Tahoe night still lurked The Terror.

Waiting up for Nona to come home from her date took me back to her teenage years. I had to admit I was guilty as charged of being an overprotective mother, but I'd never had more reason to be. It's hard to tell with a basset, but I'd have sworn Cruiser looked worried, too.

I tried to distract myself by transcribing notes for an article, but I couldn't concentrate. Then I studied my new volume of "Writer's Market." I sat on the couch stroking Cruiser as I flipped through the pages absently. It was no use. I couldn't think of anything but Nona. Where was my daughter? Was she all right?

Nearly 2:00 A.M. and still no sign of them. I was determined to wait up until Nona returned safely home. In the warmth of the fire's waning glow, I fought to keep my eyelids and my favorite book "The Complete Sherlock Holmes" propped open, but I was fast losing the battle. The sensation of the book dropping heavily on my chest startled me back to consciousness once or twice, then soon the print grew fuzzy before my eyes...

I dreamed I wandered on a dark, lonely moor. A piercing wind wailed like a lost soul in the vast expanse as clouds sailed the undulating landscape like ghost ships. I tugged the flaps of my deerstalker tight around my ears. As I trekked through the shaggy bracken, the cold stare of a winter moon was a dead man's eye in the night. Fear clutched my heart when I heard a strange rustling in the foliage. It was only my faithful scent hound on the trail of our quarry. Suddenly, Cruiser lifted his nose into the air and began to bay. The chase was on. My hound's sonorous bawl echoed across the moor as I tripped on the crumbled stone arteries of Caesar's legions. Faster I ran down dale and across bubbling ford. I felt the icy water on my feet, then the scene transformed...

I found myself ankle deep in fresh snow, surrounded by majestic firs. I was no longer on the wild moors of England but in a deep forest. I glimpsed in the distance the light of my own cabin, a dim but comforting glow in the velvet darkness. My feet sank in the powder as the full moon, now a menacing feral orb in the night sky, peered at me through the branches of the pines. The Big Dipper spilled buckets of sparkling white diamonds across the firmament to guide me, and also the beast tracking its prey. I sensed it drawing closer. Closer. I felt its damp, hot breath upon the nape of my neck. I dared not look behind me for fear of what I might see. I could only run. Run for my life.

All at once, I had caught up with Cruiser and found myself at the foot of Cave Rock. Cruiser froze in a point, growling. I looked up to where the moon shone on the glittering, granite monolith. There stood an enormous snarling beast, whiter than the new-fallen snow. It seemed strangely iridescent in the brightness of the moon, foam dripping from its blood-red maw.

In the moonglow, I saw a lifeless form being torn and tossed. "Nona!" When I screamed, the creature dropped its prey and emitted a soul-splintering wail before leaping high into the air. A quicksilver mass blotted the moon and

stars from my sight for an instant before...
      I jolted awake in my armchair, crying out Nona's name. Cruiser planted his paws on my chest and licked my face. My Sherlock anthology lay open on the floor to page 669, "The Hound of the Baskervilles."

Chapter Twenty-seven

Sunlight streaming through my bedroom window hit my eyes like a laser. I rubbed the sleep from my peepers, still trying to remember when I had finally hit the hay the night before. Everything seemed confused in my mind. Had Nona really gone on a date with Medwyn? Had I dreamed what happened at Cave Rock, or was it as real as it seemed? When I stretched and my toes hit the lump of snoring basset at the foot of my bed, the lingering shadows dispersed.

Every muscle ached as I swung my feet from under the covers and touched them to the floor.

"Come on, Cruiser. Time to rise and shine. "Let's go get some breakfast, boy."

I tiptoed down the hall to check on Nona. She must have had a very late night, since I hadn't heard her come in. But I could sleep like a hibernating bear. Besides, I knew she would have tried to be quiet if she were coming in so late. Tom and I had raised a considerate daughter.

Her door was ajar, so I pushed it gently. I winced as it squeaked loudly. How many times had I meant to squirt a little WD-40 on those noisy hinges? That's one of the problems about living alone and manless. Tom always took care of all those little things. Without him, squeaks and leaks never seemed to get fixed. I was always too busy writing or sniffing out crime scenes with Skip, like Cruiser sniffed around the kitchen floor, looking for errant morsels from last night's supper.

The guest room was quiet. Too quiet. Nona was a feather-light sleeper, and those squeaky hinges would surely have roused her. I heard no rustling of bed covers as I pushed the door the rest of the way open, hinges squealing like a mouse caught in a trap. I felt my heart do double-time in my

chest when I saw Nona's bed still unslept in. I knew she had
to leave for San Francisco this morning, but would she have
left without telling me? Had I said or done something to
make her that angry? No. It wasn't Nona's style to just take
a powder. Even if she were furious with me, she would never
have left without saying a proper good-bye. Tom's untimely
death had taught us always to part company with a loved one
like it's the last time you'll ever see them, because it may
well be.

Her bags were sitting unpacked in the corner. I felt
my stomach knot when I realized Nona had never come home
from her date with Medwyn. I shuddered as I remembered
my vivid nightmare. I felt slightly better when I discovered
Nona's missing shoe, which had fallen behind her suitcase.
I placed it back in the Nieman Marcus shoe box with its
mate. Now only Nona was still missing. The knot in my
stomach tightened.

"Nona! Are you here? Answer me!" Cruiser followed close at my heels as I checked room after room. The
house was more silent than ever before. I flopped down in
Tom's chair as I fought back a flood of tears. How could I
have let her go out last night? It was my gut feeling that
Silvernail was no more the Tahoe Terror than Cruiser, which
meant the killer was still out there somewhere, and so was
Nona. As I verbally flagellated myself, Cruiser looked up at
me, concerned about all the noise I made. As usual, I spoke
to him as though he were a person in the absence of the real
thing.

"What's wrong with me? How could I be so stupid?" I railed. "Stupid, stupid, stupid!" The dam finally
burst. "Oh, Nona! Where are you?" Tears spilled down my
face, wetting my robe and splashing on Cruiser. As I sobbed,
I grew aware of a gentle tongue upon my hand. Cruiser
whined in sympathy. I stroked his head. "Thanks, boy."
I'd swear that Cruiser's sad brown eyes teared up, too.

"This is silly. I'm overreacting." I stopped crying
and wiped my eyes on my bathrobe sleeve. "Nona can take
care of herself. Why am I getting so upset over a silly dream?
That's all it was. Just a dream."

I jumped when the phone rang. It was Skip.

"Hey, Beanie."

"Hey, Skip. What's up?" I sniffled.

"There's been another killing."

My throat froze with fear as I realized what his next words might be. Finally I managed to hoot, "Wh...Wh...Who?"

"Another Tallis employee."

I sighed, relieved it wasn't Nona. "Jeez, which one this time?"

"William Trevor. An assistant administrator."

"The killer must be working his way down the org chart."

"This one is the same MO as the first ones. We also know for sure it's not Dan Silvernail."

"I hate to say I told you so, but I told you so. What finally convinced you?"

"His alibi checked out. We located his girlfriend."

"And she corroborated his story?"

"Yes. He was where he said at the time Brennan was killed. We're releasing him this morning."

"Have you talked to Stoddard, yet?"

"Not yet."

"Why not?"

"He's missing. Walked right out of the hospital."

"We have to find out who our perp is and *now!*" I said. "We have another problem."

"What?"

A Cave Rock-sized lump in my throat choked my words.

"Beanie, you all right?"

"Uh, huh."

"You sound kinda funny. Do you have a cold?"

"No."

"What's wrong, then?"

"It's Nona," I blubbered. "She didn't come home last night."

"That's not so unusual for an independent gal like Nona."

"She was out with Medwyn, Skip."

"So?"

"Nona would never stay out all night when she's visiting me without calling. She even had her cellular phone with her. Something must be terribly wrong."

"Maybe the battery wasn't charged. Calm down."

"I don't like this, Skip. I don't like it at all."

"Why don't you come over to the station, and we'll get a missing person's report started."

"I'll be there as soon as I can. I just have to throw some food in Cruiser's bowl and yank on some clothes."

"Try not to worry too much, Beanie. I'm sure Nona'll turn up."

Skip's tone didn't sound the least bit reassuring. Besides, there was plenty to worry about. And worry I would.

I spilled some kibble into Cruiser's dish, unfastened the dog door so he could get out to do his business, then spread some newspapers on the floor just in case he couldn't. I didn't take time to shower but just splashed the sleep from my eyes with cold water. I slipped on my jeans and sweatshirt and raked a brush through my hair. Within ten minutes, I was racing down the highway.

I skidded into the parking lot and came to a screeching halt outside the Sheriff's office. I ran to the door, nearly slipping on the patches of black ice on the asphalt. It wouldn't have been the first time since I'd moved here that I landed right on my butt on icy pavement, but this time I skated to the door and gripped the handle just in the nick of time.

"Hey, don't you guys ever salt your parking lot? I almost did a triple toe loop getting to your front door just now."

"Sorry, Oksana," Skip said through the steam rising from his morning coffee. "I guess we slipped up."

"No. I'm the one who slipped."

"Here, Beanie, why don't you fill this out for me."

I glanced down at the missing persons form. I started to choke up again. "Oh, Skip, where on earth can Nona be?"

"Simmer down. It's too soon to panic."

"For you, maybe. She's not your daughter."

"Have you considered the fact that she might have run off with Medwyn?"

"No, I hadn't considered that possibility."

"She knew you couldn't stand the guy."

"This is true." Skip's explanation comforted me only momentarily. He was right; Nona has a rebellious streak.

Could she have run off with Medwyn to marry him? Now that really was an awful thought.

Skip handed me a pen. "Go ahead and fill this out, okay? It'll help us find Nona faster."

It's customary to wait at least 48 hours before filing a missing persons report. I was grateful to Skip for bending the rules for a friend.

"Could you get me a cup of coffee?" I asked as I began filling in the blanks on the form. "I didn't have time for any this morning."

"Sure thing. Be right back."

Height, 5'8"; Weight, 125 lbs.; Hair, black; Eyes, brown. The general descriptions didn't do her justice. Her hair is chestnut, not dark brown. Her eyes are ginger spice. As I wrote, I remembered holding my daughter for the first time after she was born, wrapped in the flannel baby blanket with teddy bears on it, a shower gift from my mother. I could still see the cap of delicate, reddish-brown curls on her tiny head and smell the pink cloud baby scent of her soft, golden skin. How my arms ached to hold her, the woman, not the baby. The baby was only a memory.

Nona. Missing! The full weight of the situation hit me again like a brick. As I finished writing and laid down the pen, I prayed the woman wouldn't be only a memory, too.

Skip reappeared carrying two coffee cups. He handed one to me. "Here's your coffee."

"Thanks. I'm finished with this. Now can we get this cart and pony show on the road?"

"Sure thing. Just call me P.T. Barnum." Skip handed the completed form to his assistant, Pam. "Do you have a recent photo of Nona?"

I fished in my purse and pulled out my wallet. Luckily, the snapshot of Nona I handed to him was taken only a month ago. Thank goodness it wasn't from her Victoria's Secret modeling gig.

"This is a great photo of her! She looks like a movie star."

"She's always been photogenic, unlike her mother."

"I'll scan it into the computer and fax it along with the report."

"I'm scared, Skip. I know my daughter wouldn't just not turn up without calling me, even if she had to hunt for a pay phone."

"We'll find her, Beanie. I promise."

But in what condition would we find her? I knew Skip and the Sheriff's Department would do everything within their power to search for my missing daughter, but in the meantime this sleuth and her scent hound weren't going to sit around nervously scarfing chocolate chip cookies and dog biscuits while Nona was Heaven knows where.

Chapter Twenty-eight

I drove toward home in a kind of daze, steering the car but not really seeing the road. After I picked up Cruiser, we would search every spot where Nona might be, starting at Medwyn's house. Cruiser's keen nose would finally be used for something besides sniffing out treats from the yum-yum nook. A basset's sense of smell is second only to a bloodhound's, and I needed all the help I could get. I knew one thing, the sooner I found Nona, the better the chance I would find her unharmed, and unmarried.

When I pulled into the driveway, the sight of Nona's little Volkswagen stabbed at my heart. Where was my daughter? I silently vowed if I was lucky enough to find her alive, I would heed my instincts about Nona's welfare in the future. I should have pleaded with her or hog-tied her, if necessary. And I should have kept her away from that rat, Medwyn. I blamed myself for her disappearance, as I had over Tom's fate.

The sun was a 25-watt bulb in the flannel gray sky as Cruiser and I ascended winding Kingsbury Grade. I finally found the address I had seen on the Tallis org chart under Medwyn's name, but the name on the mailbox read Millicent Drury. Who was Millicent Drury? I followed a gravel road for a good two miles off the main highway until I came to a ranch-style house. I pulled into a circular drive and got out of my Jeep. The place seemed deserted. One way to find out for sure. Cruiser leapt out when I opened the passenger door.

"Come on, Cruiser. Let's check it out, boy." Cruiser's nose kissed the ground and stuck there like a magnet. He tracked the scent he'd picked up and quickly disappeared around the side of the house.

I walked up to the porch and rang the doorbell. I heard dogs barking out back, but no one came to the door. I rang once more.

"Hello!" I knocked on the door. "Anyone home?" Still no response. I walked to the picture window and peered inside through cupped hands. I gasped at the sight. Newspapers lined every inch of the floor, and empty feeders dotted the room. The carpet was matted and stained. In one corner I saw a cardboard box piled high with what appeared to be old clothes or shoes. When I walked around the side of the house to find Cruiser, the odor of urine and feces assaulted my nose. I stood stunned at what I saw: cage after filthy, crowded cage of pit bulls, rottweilers, mastiffs leaping and snarling in a deafening cacophony of canine misery and neglect. Kennel rage at its worst. A forlorn mastiff bitch lay listless on her side, jutting ribs heaving as a dozen pups wriggled at her side nudging teats for milk that wouldn't come. There was no mistaking what I'd stumbled onto. I knew Cruiser and I had disliked Medwyn for good reason, but I never dreamed he was operating a puppy mill.

Satisfied Nona wasn't at Medwyn's place, I continued my search, more disturbed than ever by what I had found. I'd have to report this to the authorities. Something would have to be done about those pathetic animals, but first I had to find my daughter. I drove from Spooner Lake to Emerald Bay, cruising past every spot Nona and I had ever been from the time she was a toddler. Cruising right along beside me, ears flapping in the breeze, his keen nose catching every scent, was my basset buddy.

As we passed through Cave Rock, I honked the horn, as Tom always did when Nona was little. She loved that. The echo in the 200-foot tunnel seemed different today. As the sound trailed off, I fancied I heard the woeful cries of imprisoned Washoe spirits welling from deep in the cavern the white man buried when he bored this tunnel through our sacred stone. Or was it something far more menacing I heard echoing through the cave? As I drove through the tunnel into the light, I scanned the roadside for any sign of my lost daughter. I interrogated acquaintances and then complete strangers on Nona's whereabouts.

"Sorry, I haven't seen her, Beanie," Bob said when I stopped at the fire station. The story was the same from Sally at the Haute Hydrant, Jim at Wildlife Rescue, and everyone else I asked. No one had seen Nona. Every familiar landmark looked cold and deserted beneath the blanket of snow. Would I ever see my daughter again?

I walked Cruiser along the stretch of woods at Kiva Beach where only days ago Nona and I had skied together. This day looked similar, with its charcoal-smudged sky and intermittent snow flurries. The lake was as gray as the canopy above; white mounds of snow and ice along her shallows brought to mind Kanuwapi's great, white bear rising up from the lake.

I saw a string of Canada geese as I had that day. I thought their calls sounded beautiful when Nona was here. Now they seemed as hollow and melancholy as I felt. The pain in my heart grew almost unbearable as I watched them glide farther down the shore and out of sight. Like my daughter, something beautiful had disappeared from my vision. I wanted the geese to come back, as if somehow they could bring her back with them. In a sudden flurry, they took flight, scattering diamonds of water in their wake. I wondered if they carried the soul of my daughter up to the Great Spirit on their wings. The sounds of their honking faded as the V of geese, silhouetted against the gray sky, shrank smaller and smaller on the horizon, then finally out of sight.

I passed the spot where we had found the hunter's body when we were skiing, and the horror of the serial killings and the realization I might find my daughter in the same condition stabbed my heart like an ice pick. I stopped in my tracks and, like Cruiser, inhaled the cold air and heady incense of the woods. I watched his head bobbing as each scent telegraphed its message through his sensitive nose. The crisp oxygen provided an elixir to my fevered brain. I began to rehash all the events since this madness began.

I sat down on the same log where Nona and I had lunched together. Cruiser sniffed a nearby tree, honing in for a hosing. Tears slipped from under my lashes and froze in tiny waterfalls on my cheeks. Over the past centuries, how many tears had the Washoe shed over the destruction of their beautiful alpine home? Like snowflakes, they could never be counted. My tears on this snowy day were shed not only for the loss of the Washoe Tribe's way of life but for fear of forever losing Nona, whose fate hung in the balance like the fate of this valley, its deepening scars hidden by winter's soft white cloak.

Chapter Twenty-nine

"You're going to have to lay off the French fries, boy," I gasped, hefting Cruiser back into his copilot's seat. "Doc Heaton's going to have a hissy fit, not to mention a hernia, next time he lifts you onto his examination table." I slammed the door, first ensuring all appendages were tucked safely inside. I rolled down the passenger window, and immediately a moist, black nose popped out, poised and ready for action.

We were back to square one. I had driven from one end of the basin to the other, but Nona was nowhere to be found. The sun dipped below the rim of the purple peaks. Soon darkness would shroud the mountains. I was exhausted, with not a clue of where to go from here, but I would resume my search at first light. When I got back to the cabin, I dialed Skip's office to see if anything had turned up, like my missing daughter.

"Sheriff's Office, Cassidy."

"Hey, Skip, it's me."

"Has Nona shown up?"

"Nope. Any news there, yet?"

"No. Now, try not to worry, Beanie."

"I'm trying, I'm trying. Cruiser and I have looked everywhere, and there's no sign of her. We even went to Medwyn's. You won't believe what we found there."

"I'm all ears. Oops, I forgot. Cruiser's line."

"Please, this is no time for your lame jokes."

"Sorry. Just trying to cheer you up. What did you find?"

"A puppy mill."

"Where is his place?"

"At a ranch, located a couple of miles off of

Kingsbury Grade. I know I had Medwyn's correct address, but there was another name on the mailbox. Millicent Drury."

"Could have been his mother's name," said Skip.

"Yeah, he said she died recently." Of natural causes, I hoped. I shivered as I thought again of that awful place.

"Who knows? This guy's a pretty cool customer."

"No wonder he didn't want anyone to know where he lived. The inside of the house is disgusting, but the kennels are worse. Those poor animals need help."

"It'll be taken care of, but in the meantime, I think we'd better find your daughter and pronto. I'll have a search party together within the hour."

I felt relieved that an all out search had begun for Nona. I wanted to go along, but Skip advised me to stay at home in case she turned up. Cruiser seemed as glad as I to be back at the cabin, but the place seemed so empty without Nona there. I wadded up some newspapers and placed kindling and several logs on the grate. I struck a match to the paper and within minutes, a comforting flame roared in the fireplace.

I sank into Tom's easy chair. Cruiser seemed to sense my loneliness and discouragement. Instead of heading for his hairy pillow on the couch, he ambled over and laid his jowls on my knee, a great sacrifice for a couch spud like him. He didn't even check out the food bowl in the kitchen. Cruiser got a leg-up on the ottoman and licked my hand. I stroked his head. His soft, warm coat felt pleasant beneath my cold fingers. As always, he offered comfort when it is most needed. I patted a hand on my lap, and he climbed the rest of the way up. With my arm draped over Cruiser and his chin on my chest, we soon dozed in the fire's warmth.

The crack of a log startled me awake. A glowing shower of sparks spit like an angry cat. At least I thought that's the sound that woke me. I glanced at the clock on the mantle beneath my grandfather's bow and arrows. It was nearly midnight. The firelight flickered on the razor sharp tips of the arrows. I thought of how Grandfather first taught me to shoot by placing pinecones in a line on a rock. By the time I was ten years old, I could have shot the fleas off a squirrel, or a basset, at 100 yards. The chiming clock scattered my memories like wild geese before the storm.

Cruiser no longer lay on my lap. Probably doing sentry duty at the food dish. After all, it was time for his midnight snack. Anytime was snack time, especially for a land shark like Cruiser.

I yawned and stretched, then stood to stir the embers. The flames rose like a phoenix to consume the last few chunks of wood on the grate. As I shuffled toward the kitchen, I heard a scratching sound coming from the back door. I felt the hairs on the nape of my neck salute. Had the beast that had carved the grooves in my door returned?

I sighed with relief when I saw Cruiser scratching and whining to be let out. I had forgotten to unlock his dog door again. Poor guy had probably been standing there doing the pee-pee dance for the past hour with me snoring away blissfully in the next room.

"Hey, fella. Why didn't you come and bite me on the ankle or something?" I reached down to unlock the latches on the dog door when I heard a sound that froze us both on the spot. Cruiser tilted his nose to the ceiling and bayed but was cut off in mid-howl by my hands clamping gently over his muzzle. "Ssh, boy," I said as I strained to hear the sound emanating from deep in the forest. A woman screamed.

"Nona!" I cried. "It's Nona!"

When I opened the door, Cruiser bolted for the woods with more gusto than I had ever seen him muster, even for a Bacon Beggin' Strip. I knew where he was headed—straight for Cave Rock.

"Cruiser, come back!" I cried. I ran for the phone and dialed Skip at the sheriff's office. I prayed he would still be on duty.

"Sheriff's office, Cassidy."

"Skip! Thank God you're there. I know where Nona is. Meet me at Cave Rock. And bring some backup. I'm headed there now."

"Beanie, wait..." Skip's voice fell on dead air as the receiver swung like a pendulum from its cradle. I donned my coat and deerstalker and was out the door, clutching the flashlight in one hand and my only weapon, Grandfather's bow and arrows, in the other.

My breath froze on the air as I huffed up the incline, following Cruiser's tracks in the snow. The snowdrifts were bound to slow him up a little.

"Barooooo!" When I heard Cruiser howling in the woods just ahead of me, I knew I was catching up. In the beam of the flashlight, I saw my lop-eared sleuth chugging like a train, steam puffing from his nostrils as he tracked the scent on the moonlit trail toward Cave Rock.

I tripped over a branch and fell to my knees in the snow. I thought I saw something move among an aspen grove. I was thankful I carried Grandfather's bow and arrows. The leaves of the trees rattled like a skeleton's bones in the icy gusts of wind stabbing at my ears. I pulled the flaps of my deerstalker down and tied them tightly under my chin.

When we had nearly reached the pinnacle, I stopped to catch my breath, rising on the frigid air like smoke signals. Somewhere in the forest a startled hawk answered the shriek of terror, then a gunshot ripped the night. I ran faster, following the sound of a terrible commotion.

Cave Rock was cloaked in cloud shadows on the snowy clearing before me. Far below, the lake mirrored the quicksilver ether. Cruiser had frozen in a point at my side. High above, an owl brushed the tips of the pines with its outstretched wings. Then the full moon slipped from behind the clouds, revealing a yawning crevasse at the side of snow-capped Cave Rock, a grinning skull in the ghostly moonlight.

I spotted in a snowdrift at the base of the rock a figure lying face down. An icy dread clutched my heart as I recalled my terrible nightmare. I heard a man's deep, gurgling moan, then silence. When I turned the body over, the moonlight struck Medwyn's face. Blood oozed from a deep wound on his neck. I noticed the pistol half buried in the snow beside him, the pungent smell of gunpowder hanging in the night air. I prayed I wasn't too late to save Nona. I tensed when Cruiser growled, his attention trained somewhere above me. Then I heard the ominous rumbling sound.

Chapter Thirty

I glanced up. There on the massive granite tor stood absolutely the largest specimen of Canis familiaris I have ever seen. I stared in disbelief at the sheer size of its pure white body, which shimmered strangely in the moonlight. When I heard the low rumble rise up from its barrel-sized chest, I realized the ghastly creature was all too real. It was the most terrifying sight I'd ever laid eyes on. The head was massive. Bloody saliva hung in gory threads from its enormous jaws. I saw its flanks stiffen at Cruiser's frenzied barking. "Shh, Cruiser. No, boy." He quieted momentarily, then set in again.

I dared not run, or I was a dead woman. What could I do? To my horror, Cruiser lunged. "Cruiser, NO!" With his stubby legs, his attempts to reach the brute were futile. He'd be killed for sure. Compared to the size of Medwyn's trained beast, Cruiser was a Chihuahua.

When the huge dog roared, my legs nearly folded under me. Cruiser never let up barking. The enraged animal snapped at the air, huffing hot steam through its nostrils. Snarling lips drew back from bared teeth, readied for the kill.

Shaking there in my hiking boots, I remembered my grandfather's tale of Kanuwapi, the brave warrior who slew the great bear with his arrow. I hooked an arrow into position on Grandfather's bow and pointed it at the slavering beast atop Cave Rock. A hundred times my grandfather had placed pinecones on a rock for me to shoot, and a hundred times he had guided my hands. Where was Grandfather's steadying hand now? My fingers trembled uncontrollably as I stretched the taught cord farther...farther. As I held my hand quivering at my ear, I heard the trusted murmur of

Grandfather's voice.

"Slowly, Papoose. Aim...hold..." I released.

The arrow whizzed past Cruiser and struck the creature's loin. Blood stained silver-white fur as the dog toppled from the stone and landed in the snow. In its agony, the animal lunged for Cruiser. Cruiser howled in pain as razor-sharp incisors grazed his shoulder and sent him tumbling tail over teakettle.

"Cruiser!" I cried. When he didn't respond, I feared he might be dead.

The beast spun around again to attack. I aimed another arrow and let it fly. This time the arrow pierced the animal's neck. Blood spurted from the wound and drenched the snow in crimson. The dog prepared to lunge once more, eyes glowering with blood lust. I aimed my weapon. A dreadful howl seared the chill night air as the missile found its mark.

A moment later, the forest clearing was silent, except for Cruiser whining in pain. Then I heard someone whimper nearby. I aimed my flashlight in the direction of the sound.

"Mom, is that you?"

"Nona! You're alive! Thank God."

"Mom!"

I ran to my daughter and swept her into my arms. "Oh, honey. I'm so glad you're safe." When Nona didn't hug me back, I realized her arms were bound behind her back. I loosened the knots and unraveled the cord to release her.

"Aggh! My arm. I think it's broken."

The snapping of a twig startled me. "Cruiser?"

When Nona screamed, my heart skipped a beat. In the moonlight, I saw Medwyn standing beside the impaled body of the killer dog, the pistol in his hand trained on me.

"I knew you'd turn up sooner or later. The typical interfering mother. You just couldn't leave us alone, could you?" Medwyn growled more menacingly at me than the mastiff had moments before.

"Not if Nona was in danger."

"She was never in any danger. I told you, you crazy old woman. I love her!"

What's this? He was calling *me* crazy? "Do you usually kidnap people you love?"

"You have to guard what's yours or, sure to God, someone will take it away from you."

It was the first thing Medwyn had ever said to me that made any sense. Why else would I be up at Cave Rock in the middle of the night with this madman, looking down the barrel of a .38?

"They took everything away from me that mattered. My job, my home, my life. Everything!"

"Who, Medwyn?" I was stalling. Anything to keep him talking. I had to find some way to distract him. But how?

"Those jerks at Tallis: Robson, Caruso, all of 'em. And my mother, my stepfather, everyone since the day I was born."

He'd killed his parents, too? This wasn't looking good for us. But at least his attention was diverted, until Nona groaned in pain. Medwyn's eyes locked on her, distracting him for a moment. The gun lowered slightly. The front of his shirt looked black in the moonlight. I knew it must be soaked with blood. He lost his footing a moment, then braced himself against the rock. His strength rallied and he trained the gun on me once more.

"And even you, you meddlesome witch!" I heard Cruiser growl at Medwyn's threatening tone.

"Shhh, Cruiser, boy. Stay!" I said, fearing he might be shot where he lay. Medwyn paid him no mind.

"Say good-bye to your daughter. She's mine now!"

"No, Medwyn, please..." Nona cried. I heard a click as he cocked the hammer. No time left to think of a way out. Nona was injured. If I tried to pull her out of the way, he would probably shoot her instead of me. I could think only of protecting Nona. I shielded her with my body and braced for the inevitable.

I winced as I heard a gunshot tear the night and echo through the cave, but strangely I felt no pain. So this was what death was like? I examined myself for a wound but found none. No blood issued forth from a bullet hole. I knew for sure I wasn't dead when I heard Nona shriek, but this time it wasn't from pain or terror. Medwyn dropped face-first into the snow, the gun in his fist still unfired. He didn't get up.

"Beanie!" I whirled to see Skip standing in the moonlit clearing holding his rifle and flashlight. "Are...you...all...right?" Skip's breath hitched from his run up the mountainside. Several officers flanked him.

"Skip!"

He panned his flashlight across the bloodstained snow. The beam froze a moment on Medwyn's corpse and then on the dead dog, lanced through the heart with my arrow. "What the devil happened here?"

"Uh...uh." Still stunned, I couldn't seem to string a sentence together. For once, I was at a loss for words.

"Say something, Beanie. Are you all right?"

"I...I'm fine. But Nona's hurt, and Cruiser, too. See after him, will you? I'll take care of Nona."

"Will do."

I gently touched Nona's right arm to try to determine how badly it was broken.

"Ow!" Nona cried.

"It looks like a simple fracture, but we need to keep that arm steady somehow."

"It hurts bad."

"I know, honey. Just keep it as still as you can."

"I'm trying to, Mom."

"Wait a minute, I have an idea."

I untied my deerstalker and, cradling her injured arm in the upturned cap, I knotted the ties behind her neck. "That'll hold it steady until we can get you to the hospital."

My heart could have melted all the snow on the mountain when, as I helped Nona to her feet, she planted a big, wet kiss on my cheek, like so many times in childhood when scraped knees brought her crying to me for comfort.

"How's Cruiser, Skip?" I asked.

"He's a little skinned up, but he'll live to fight another day."

Skip made snowballs to wash the blood from Cruiser's shoulder. The snow seemed to douse the fire of his wounds, for my brave warrior stopped whining.

"What a good boy," Nona said, stroking Cruiser's head with her left hand.

Nona leaned against me for support. Cruiser limped along behind.

"Skip, you'd better carry Cruiser. We'll make better headway."

"Come on, Cruiser, old buddy." I heard Skip grunt as he hefted him into his arms.

The dark pines seemed to slam shut behind us as we emerged from the mysteries and terrors of Cave Rock. The sight of the patrol cars flashing like the twinkle lights on a Christmas tree was the most comforting sight I ever saw. I slid in next to Nona in Skip's car. The warmth inside was a welcome change from our chilling adventure. Skip lifted Cruiser gently onto the front seat. As Skip climbed aboard, I couldn't help noticing that his copilot lacked his usual enthusiasm for hanging out the passenger window. Nona sighed and bumped her head against my shoulder.

"Hang on, Nonie. We'll be there soon," I clucked, stroking her hair.

"I love you, Mom."

"Me, too, Papoose."

"That's what Grandpop used to call you, isn't it?"

"Yes." As I looked out the window, I could see puffs of white clouds floating over the lake, like the smoke from Grandfather's pipe.

"Everyone okay back there?" Skip hollered over the wailing sirens.

"Just get us to a hospital and a veterinarian and we'll all be dandy. Hit the gas, Skip!"

He U-turned west on Highway 50. "We're outta here!"

Chapter Thirty-one

"*REIGN OF TERROR ENDS—TALLIS KILLER AND GIANT MASTIFF SLAIN IN CAVE ROCK SHOOTOUT. TAHOE HUMANE SOCIETY BUSTS NEVADA DOGFIGHT RING,*" read the headlines of my wrap-up article in the Tahoe Times. In the lower left corner of the front page was a photo of Mike Stoddard with the caption, **Mayoral candidate indicted for murder.**

Residents of South Lake Tahoe breathed a little easier as they drank their cups of coffee over their Sunday morning papers, including those sitting at my kitchen table.

Nona and I were having our coffee when Skip popped in early to share the good news about his promotion to acting sheriff until the next election.

"Well," Skip said, pouring himself a cup of coffee. "You really made mincemeat out of The Tahoe Terror, didn't you, Beanie, old girl."

"Watch it with the 'old girl' stuff, Skip. I don't get my A.A.R.P. card until my birthday next July."

Skip grinned. "We'll have to plan a celebration for the Big 5-0."

"The fact that this nightmare's over and Nona is safe is celebration enough for me."

"You can say that again," Nona said.

"And I'm rid of Stoddard," Skip said.

"He'll be cooling his heels in prison quite some time," I said. "Who would have thought Rita would go turncoat on her Sugar Daddy."

"Sugar Daddy?" Nona looked puzzled.

"Stoddard," Skip said. "Rita blew the whistle on him when she didn't get the wedding ring he promised her to pick Dan Silvernail out of the lineup."

"Besides, she was fed up with his dirty dog dealings, even if she didn't mind being a crooked politician's wife," I said.

"Did you know your boss was involved in a dog fight ring, Skip?" Nona asked.

"I suspected he might be up to something crooked but didn't know for sure until one day when I was in the john and heard someone come into the stall next to mine. I recognized Stoddard's size 13 boots right away."

"Those would be the same size 13s you discovered the mate to at Medwyn's hell hole of a house," I said.

"Yep, the very same. Anyway, I heard him tear something up, then flush it down the toilet. After he left, I picked up several pieces of paper on the floor."

"What was he flushing?" Nona asked.

"A torn gambling stub from the dog fights."

"Do you think he knew you were in the stall next to him?" I asked.

"Must have. Especially since he made life a living hell for me after that; I mean, more than usual. He thought he was so smart, but he didn't have anyone fooled. Medwyn duped everyone, though."

"Not Mom," said Nona. "She saw through him from the start."

"I knew I didn't like him dating my daughter, but if I'd known he was abusing dogs and training them to be killers, I'd have sicced Cruiser on him the first time he walked in my front door."

Skip and Nona laughed. King Cruiser thumped his tail on his hairy throne.

"Where did Medwyn get such a hideous dog, Mom? I never saw a dog that big before."

"That makes two of us," I said. "I saw other mastiffs at the puppy mill, but this one qualified for a Guinness world record. I think Medwyn was probably involved in some kind of experimental breeding to produce a dog that large."

"That could explain the DNA anomalies we discovered in the tissue samples," Skip said. "But it *was* an Old English mastiff. Right, Beanie?"

"Yes. The breed dates as far back as 3000 BC in

Egypt. In England, they fought alongside their masters against Caesar's army with such power and ferocity that they were brought back to perform in the Circus in Rome, where they defeated all other dog breeds, not to mention lions, tigers and bears."

"Oh, my," Skip joked.

"Thank God that nowadays responsible mastiff breeders promote a good-natured dog of more normal stature."

"Romans invented the sport of dog fighting?" Nona asked.

"Most likely, if you can call such cruelty a sport," I said.

"But what made it glow in the dark that way, Mom? It was the most terrifying thing I ever saw."

"That's exactly what Medwyn wanted. He wanted the huge dog to appear even more frightening to its victims, so he dusted its coat with a nontoxic photoactive powder that made it appear to glow."

"It worked," said Skip. "The Tallis victims all died of fright before the dog ever attacked them, except for Medwyn."

"Why would the dog would attack its own master?" Nona said.

"We don't know how Medwyn treated the dog. He may have abused it. Besides, there was probably a lot of inbreeding in the dog. That can make for an unpredictable animal."

"Like trying to reverse a Cruise missile once you launch it, huh, Mom?"

"Good analogy, but don't you mean a Cruiser missile?"

Nona laughed, petting Cruiser. "Sorry I underestimated you, fella. I'd have been a goner for sure if it weren't for you." Cruiser licked Nona's hand.

"Anyway, you don't have to worry about that beast or Medwyn any more," Skip said.

"Luckily, you finished him off before he could finish us, Skip."

"But how did Tallis fit into all this?" Nona asked.

"Tallis was having serious financial troubles. They

were way overextended. Getting a piece of the dog fight action helped them avoid filing Chapter 11 and keep the Cave Rock Project afloat."

"They certainly weren't above crooked dealings to get what they wanted," Skip interjected.

"They'd bitten off more than they could chew, and the Washoe dissent on the Cave Rock issue was complicating matters tremendously. Plus they were way overspent on Stoddard's campaign for Mayor."

"I'm glad Dan and Sonseah stood up to Tallis," Nona said.

"Me, too," I said, feeling a little guilty I hadn't been penning placards for their cause.

"Dan Silvernail knew that if Brennan helped get Stoddard elected, Stoddard would help Tallis acquire other Native lands for development," Skip said. "That's why he confronted Brennan at the meeting."

"Right," I said. "And afterward in the parking lot. He tried to persuade Brennan to kill the plans for the resort, dump Stoddard and back Thor in the election."

"Only Brennan got killed, instead." Skip poured himself another cup of coffee. "Can you pass the cream, Nona?"

"Sure, my other arm still works fine." Nona shoved the creamer toward him with her good arm. "So, Stoddard killed Brennan, not Dan Silvernail or Medwyn's dog. Right, Mom?"

"Yes."

"But why did he do it?"

"He was already cuckoo," Skip said, making corkscrew motions at his temple with an index finger. "He went off the edge when Brennan threatened to pull the plug on the campaign funds. That's why he was betting on the dogs, anything to keep his sinking campaign afloat. It was like trying to cork a leak on the Titanic."

"It would have worked out perfectly for Stoddard," I said. "Kill Brennan himself, then pin it on Silvernail. He bungled it, though."

"That's why we detected no trace of saliva or foreign tissue in Brennan's wounds," Skip added.

"Precisely."

"Anyway, I'd say Tallis is history around here, wouldn't you, Beanie?"

"I'd say so, since the Tahoe Terror pretty much wiped out the whole corporation."

"Maybe the killer dog wasn't Tahoe's real terror, though," Skip countered.

"You mean Medwyn?"

"Well, him too. But I meant my boss, or I should say, ex-boss. Stoddard was determined to be mayor and didn't care who or what he destroyed in the process."

"He was also concerned that Brennan might shelve the Cave Rock Project," I added. "That was Stoddard's election platform, remember? 'Scale the Peaks for Progress.' Hah!"

"Cave Rock Resort would have been just the beginning of more environmental troubles for Tahoe, huh, Mom?"

"Absolutely."

"What was Medwyn's beef with Tallis, though?" Nona queried.

"Revenge. Pure and simple."

"Tallis had started downsizing to make ends meet," Skip said. "Where have I heard that word before?"

"And they downsized Medwyn," I added. "They were probably funding the whole doggy operation, but when they let Medwyn go, he turned it all against them."

"Bad mistake on their part firing Medwyn," Skip said. "They didn't know who they were dealing with. He even set the beast on his stepmother when she threatened to expose his dog fight operation."

"Although she certainly wasn't above making money off of her puppy mill by selling dogs to pet shops," I said.

"We found her buried in a shallow grave in the woods behind the kennels."

"What about his stepfather?" Nona asked.

"He died several years ago."

"I'd wager that Medwyn bumped him off, too, if you did some checking, Skip."

"Could have had a grudge against him, too, I suppose." Skip said. "With these psycho types, you never know how far back the troubles go."

"Medwyn was probably cruel to animals even as a

child. Abusing animals as a youngster is an early warning sign of criminal behavior in adulthood."

"For all we know, he may have been abused himself," Skip added.

"Possibly, or maybe just plain bad to the bone, right Cruiser?" I stroked my basset buddy, and he licked my hand in agreement.

"How could I have been so blind about him? You saw through Medwyn from the very first, didn't you, Mom?"

"No, I think our friend Cruiser here was the first, but I probably wouldn't have liked Medwyn if he'd come gift-wrapped with a gingham bow, even if he hadn't had designs on marrying my daughter."

"Better dead than wed, huh?" Skip laughed.

"It's just as well," I said. "Tahoe was going to the dogs. Sorry, Cruiser."

"But what about the missing shoes?" Nona asked.

"Well..." Skip and I both spoke in unison.

"Be my guest, Ms. Sherlock," he said.

"Elementary, my dear daughter. Medwyn was training his killer dog to attack by scent."

"Too bad he never got hold of my gym sneakers," Skip joked. "Medwyn's hell hound would have dropped dead on the spot."

"Why did he come after you, Mom?"

"He wanted me out of the way. He knew I was onto him."

"I still don't understand why he wanted to kill me," Nona frowned.

"I don't think he did, honey. In his own warped way, Medwyn loved you. He wanted you for himself. I was the one he wanted out of the picture because he knew I was about to expose him. He knew I'd come running when you disappeared. You were used as bait to lure me into his trap, except it backfired on him. He was destroyed by his own creation."

"Bull mastiff bait, you mean." Nona shivered.

"I'm glad I found you in time." I hugged Nona, being careful not to bump her cast.

"Me, too, Mom."

"Well, at least the Mayoral election is in the bag for

Thor now," Skip said.

"He's got my vote. Think you'll be running for sheriff, Skip?"

"Can I count on your vote if I do?"

"Of course, and Cruiser's, too."

We all laughed when Cruiser shook his head, ears flapping and slobber flying.

"Say, how are Cruiser's wounds doing?"

"Doc Heaton treated the cuts on his shoulder. He said they're just superficial and should heal quickly. You'll hardly notice the scar two weeks from now. We take him back then to have the stitches removed. The Doc gave him a rabies shot. Just a precaution in case the mastiff was rabid."

"Good thing. We wouldn't want Cruiser to end up like Old Yeller," Skip joked.

Poor Cruiser," I crooned, stroking his head. "Him's been through a lot, hasn't him?"

You bet your biscuits him has, Cruiser seemed to say as he licked at his owie. *Just bury me at Wounded Knee— make that Wounded Shoulder.*

"Honestly, Mother," Nona said. You baby talk that dog something awful."

"Well, my poor fella's been through an awful lot the past few days. He deserves a little babying."

"We've all been through a lot," Nona said.

"Say, are you going to need help packing your bags?"

"No, thanks. I managed all right with my one good arm. I'm packed and ready to fly out of here."

"When does your plane leave?"

"In an hour. I'll have to leave my car with you until I can come back up here to get it. Probably Christmas. Is that okay, Mom?"

"Of course, but how will you get around in the meantime?"

"I may have to take BART for awhile. I can't drive too well with a broken arm."

"Yeah, you'd have to hold your cellular with your foot."

"Very funny, Mother."

"Just promise me you'll be a little more careful who you date from now on, okay?"

"Don't worry. I wouldn't want to meet up with another Medwyn."

"That makes two of us, honey."

"You can make that four, counting me and Cruiser," Skip added.

Ironically, the evil that had terrorized the valley had rid Tahoe of some of the bad people who sought to destroy her remaining beauty, but ultimately that would not be enough to save her. Nor would the scrapping of Tallis Corporation's Cave Rock Project and the company's impending bankruptcy. It was up to everyone, including the President of the United States, to ensure our splendid Jewel of the Sierras would not become forever tarnished.

"Could someone drive me to the airport?" Nona asked, fumbling with her cast as she set down her coffee cup.

"I'll take you, Nona," said Skip. "I'm headed that way, anyhow."

"I guess we'd better say our farewells here," I said. "I never could stand those Casablanca good-byes."

"Will you get my bags, Skip? They're in the guest bedroom."

"Sure thing," he said, nearly tripping over Cruiser in his eagerness.

"Better watch your step, Skip," I said. "Cruiser's the resident speed bump around here, you know."

"No kidding."

I carefully draped Nona's parka over her shoulders. "I suppose I should be the first one to autograph this, shouldn't I?" I didn't give Nona time to answer. I already had my pen poised over the plaster cast.

"Make it clever, Mom."

"Of course."

"The bags are in the car, Nona," Skip said. "All set to go?"

"Just as soon as my mother, the graffiti artist, finishes tagging my cast."

"All done," I announced.

Nona studied my drawing of Cruiser wearing my deerstalker and a Sherlock pipe hanging from his pendulous flews. "It's not the size of the hound in the fight; it's the size of the fight in the hound. Love, Mom and Cruiser."

"You're such a howl, Mother. Just like your dog."

I laughed. "Always."

"Well, gotta go. Bye, Mom," Nona said giving me a peck on the cheek.

I kissed my daughter and hugged her. "Coming up for my birthday?"

"I wouldn't miss it for the world."

"I'll try to make your future visits a bit less exciting."

"Make that *a lot* less exciting!"

"Bye, honey. Call me when you get home."

"I will, Mom. Bye."

"Love you, Nonie."

"Me, too." She blew me a kiss.

Cruiser ambled to the door and let out a bark of protest.

"Oh, sorry, Cruiser!" Nona bent down and gave him a one-armed hug. "I almost forgot to say good-bye to my hound dog hero."

I cried when Nona waved to me from Skip's car as they drove away. When she quickly turned her head, I knew she was crying, too. I waved back for as long as I thought she could see me. I'd miss her, but the time had come for me to let Nona live her own life. After all, as she said, "It *is* her life." It's called Yo-Yo Love: When you learn how to release something, it always comes back to you. I knew Nona would come back, too. As I shut the door, a fine mist of rain fell from the graying sky and turned to snow.

That night, I sat in Tom's easy chair beside a roaring fire. Cruiser was perched on his favorite hairy pillow, with his raining cats and dogs quilt tucked around him. He would play on my sympathies until his wound was completely healed. No matter. My brave boy deserved champagne and canine caviar.

Nona phoned to tell me she had arrived home safely. The reign of the Tahoe Terror had ended, and my bow and arrows were once more proudly displayed over the fireplace. Grandfather would have been surprised to know that I aimed his arrows at something bigger than a pine cone—a lot bigger! I would never intentionally hurt a dog, or any other animal, but in this case it was either us or him. The mastiff would have had to be destroyed, anyway. A dog trained to kill a human could never be anyone's devoted companion again. The puppy mill was shut down for good. I would work along with the Tahoe Humane Society in the following months to treat, socialize and place into loving homes as many of those poor dogs as could be saved. Mostly, I was thankful Nona had been saved.

As for the unfortunate climber whose tattered body had been found at the foot of Cave Rock before all the mountain mayhem began, the cause of his death would never be discovered. But I had a strong hunch. There are some things about this Lake of the Sky for which the White Man will never have explanations.

Reading my volume of Conan Doyle in the warmth of the blazing fire, I felt contented and drowsy. All seemed once more right with my world. Cruiser's steady snoring had nearly lulled me to sleep when I fancied I heard a wailing rise above the shrill winter wind. I gazed out the window of my well-lit cabin into a night as dark and deep as the mysterious lake of this ancient valley, where the restless spirits of my ancestors abide. Wah-she-shue, edeh-weeh-deeh-geh-eeh — Da-ow-a-ga.

Author Sue Owens Wright wouldn't be bothered at all if you said her literary career is going to the dogs. She adores dogs and loves writing about them. Her pup fiction, creative non-fiction and dog-gerel have appeared in The Bark; Dog Fancy; Byline; Good Dog!; Dogs International; and Pets, Part of the Family among others.

Sue makes her debut as a mystery novelist and cover illustrator with HOWLING BLOODY MURDER, the first book in a series that features-you guessed it -a dog; namely, a basset hound. Bassets are something the author knows a lot about. She's had six, five of which were rescued from pounds and shelters. She's also hosted an annual basset hound picnic in Northern California, where she lives with her husband and two bassets, Daisy and Bubba Gump.

Sue is a senior columnist for Comstock's Business magazine, which nominated her for the American Legion Auxiliary "Heart of America" Award. She studied fiction writing at Trinity College and University Galway in Ireland and University College London in England. She is a member of The Authors Guild, Mystery Writers of America, Dog Writers Association of America, PEO International, and Sisters in Crime.

Printed in the United States
6596